DEMONESS DREAMS

Wytchfae 6

Flossie Benton Rogers

Moonspell Books

Moonspell Books

Paranormal Fantasy Romance

Demoness Dreams (Wytchfae 6)

Copyright © 2022 Flossie Benton Rogers

Print ISBN: 978-0-9968439-9-7

E-book Publication: May 2015; June 2018

First Print Publication: October 2022

Cover design by Dawné Dominique

PUBLISHER

Moonspell Books

Dedication

To my husband, Ronnie, my heart. We dreamed together.

DEMONESS

DREAMS

Wytchfae 6

Flossie Benton Rogers

Chapter One

Underworld, Modern Day

Hell was the last place Bane Heughar wanted to visit. When the Goddess of the Underworld summoned, you never knew whether it was for tea and scones or to scourge you bloody. Maybe you'd get out in one piece, or maybe twelve. The pulse in his throat thudded at the sight of Helle's grim expression.

The tautness of her face indicated disturbing emotions rippling beneath the surface. Her flaxen hair framed strong cheekbones, and her wintry grey eyes glittered. She reminded him of one of her showcase fountains—an icy lake with fiery jets that spurted upward and then crashed in startling and unpredictable abandon.

Stern looking soldiers flanked her.

She extended the tips of her fingers. "Warrior." The scent of jasmine wafted into his nostrils.

He bowed his head to bestow a respectful kiss. "Goddess Helle. How may I be of service?"

"Come with me." She swiveled, and a bodyguard advanced beside her. She thrust out a palm. "Halt! You shall remain here."

The uniformed man appeared bewildered. "But Goddess, your safety is my utmost responsibility. I beg you—"

Her visage turned thunderous. "Stay, I say. I will speak to the warrior in private."

Beckoning for Bane to follow, she led him beyond the entryway of her palace, past her abode and deep into the tunnels of her cavernous domain. The pathways wound around until he doubted even his well-honed sense of direction could extricate him if she left him to find his own way.

What did she have to discuss with him that her own trusted guard could not hear?

A surge of adrenaline sizzled throughout his body. He had never ventured this far inside Helle's mysterious netherworld. She appeared to be leading him deep into one of her innermost sanctums.

At last they came to a rounded crystal enclave where gleaming spears of quartz grew in wild abandon from the rocky walls and ceiling. The crystal luminescence created a dazzling bombardment amid the strategically situated torchlights. The power generated in the room heated his blood until his ears pounded. He cleared his throat to alleviate the pressure.

Helle made her way to a great tripodal cauldron perched on an array of low rocks. "Salamander fae, forged of earth's blood, ye living fire, be at peace."

She fluttered her fingers, leaving a shimmering ripple in the air.

The flames beneath the tripod curled blue tendrils around the edges. Bane stepped closer. The tiny salamander fae, tenders of the sacred element, faded into the shadows, giving way to the Goddess. Their movement resounded in the enclave like the faint whispers of hissing steam.

The Goddess Helle swirled her hands back and forth over the cauldron and recited a strange incantation.

Even with his magical fae ability to understand foreign tongues, Bane couldn't make out all the words. *The language probably died out before humanoids rose on two limbs.*

The water in the ancient cauldron churned and spewed in the presence of the Goddess of the Underworld. A shape formed in the vessel. The image blurred with the movement of the liquid and then stilled to reveal a stunning face. The woman's hair glimmered like a halo of spun gold. A light kindled her exquisite features as if she looked upon a dazzling sight. A pleasurable thrill thrummed in the middle of

Bane's chest. When he spoke, his voice came out a whisper. "Who is she?"

Helle's tone became cold and distant. "This is the visage of a Wytchfae named Neva Jaxony, my niece and daughter of my vile, repudiated sister Skada."

Skada's sinister and sadistic exploits were well known to him, as he had cleaned up quite a few of the political tangles and murderous plots she had left behind when Helle imprisoned her. Countless dead bodies and ruined lives remained in the wake of the dark sorceress. "I didn't know Skada had a daughter."

"It is not a matter of common knowledge. However, that is she."

Bane gazed down at the vision shimmering in the dark waters of the cauldron. He wouldn't expect the daughter of such a powerful sorceress as Skada to appear so innocent. A half-smile quivered on the girl's full lips. He could almost see the stars in her eyes as if she viewed some beautiful scene. He clamped his lips together to keep from uttering an appreciative grunt. He had an inkling the powerful Goddess beside him wouldn't look favorably on such a reaction.

He glanced from the face in the water to that of the Goddess who had summoned him here and then back again into the dark depths of the cauldron. He frowned in concentration. "The girl rather favors you, Goddess Helle, in shape of face and form. Similar eyes, similar flaxen hair…though yours is somewhat lighter."

The formidable Goddess of the Underworld turned a fierce gaze upon him. "I do not appreciate the comparison, warrior. The fact that a visage comparable to mine may bring the pyres of ruin upon us is not pleasing to me in the least."

"What makes you think Neva Jaxony is a threat to the Underworld?"

"Because she is Skada's daughter and now of an age where she will start coming into her power."

"But your sister didn't raise the girl. Your niece has been kept well away from the evil that is Skada."

"My sister's blood runs through her veins, as does that of her loathsome father. Blood will always tell, warrior. You know that as well as I do. Neva turns twenty-five in a few weeks. With the onslaught of summer solstice, her quickening will be triggered by the planetary alignment, and it will be too late to stop the transformation."

He stared at Neva Jaxony's image. What crappy misfortune for such an eyeful to be so cursed. "What is the nature of the transformation?"

"The energy of the solstice will activate her blood lust. The trigger is the Solstice Moon, when the lunar body renews as crescent a few days prior to the solar alignment. If she begins to turn evil and the antidote is not administered and proven effective, her power could easily rival Skada's, if not surpass it. You must prevent the change at all costs."

Bane's brows furrowed. "I'm to dispense the antidote? What is it—a potion?"

"A potion, yes, but with an additional runic spell. The elixir must come first and have an opportunity to settle."

"I'm not a sorcerer, Goddess, just a warrior. I have no dexterity with spells, no power to make them effective."

"There are words that must be uttered, warrior, and the power is encoded. You don't need sorcery to make them work, merely a sincere heart. However, you are not the only one required to say the words that will free Skada's daughter from the evil fate that pursues her."

"Who else is needed then…a Wytchfae?"

"Not just any Wytchfae. Neva herself must say the words—either aloud or in her thoughts."

"How am I to persuade her to do that?"

"Therein lies the challenge and the crux of your task."

Bane let out a heated, shuddering breath. "Why me?"

"After your recent successful campaigns in the Underworld to corral those abhorrent creatures, the Grims, you were proclaimed Odin's warrior. A great honor, is it not?"

"One I do not merit."

"On the contrary, your attunement to our father Odin is a well-deserved reward. I now ask you to be Helle's warrior. Your skills are what I need to complete this quest. I require your subtlety and your ruthlessness. If Neva is allowed to turn demoness, she could garner greater power than her mother. She could transform into *draugr*, the female serpent dragon of the below. All the domains of the Underworld would be in danger, as well as the earth plane of humans."

"A damnable task, to be sure."

One side of her mouth lifted in a smirk. "Too much for you, warrior?"

"Not at all. You can rest assured I'll handle the matter before this girl turns evil."

Helle's pale eyes glimmered with a silvery sheen. A shadow slid behind them, causing ice to pool in Bane's stomach. "You haven't told me everything, have you, Goddess?"

The ancient and intimidating being lifted a hand, and the jewels encircling her wrist gleamed in the light from the torches that girded the magical inner sanctum. "Very astute, warrior. Perhaps I have chosen the right man for the job after all."

Bane lifted a brow and offered a direct look. "You doubt me?"

"I doubt all men when it comes to the dark forces and the womanly power my sister's blood cocoons. What runs rampant through that blood few men can resist."

Bane hesitated. He had long been curious about Helle's past but always reluctant to bring it up for fear of insulting the Goddess. Now seemed like an opportune time to ask the question that had long been puzzling him and countless others. "Forgive me for my boldness in asking such a personal question. How is it you escaped the evil that taints your sister?"

For a long moment Helle's eyes blazed, and a twitch developed in Bane's jaw. After all, she had the power to roast him to a quick cinder. Then she grunted. "All right. No harm in your question. Skada is my half-sister. We come from different mothers. Alone that wouldn't cause the disparity in our approach to life, but combine that with our differing responses to the blood call and there you pretty much have it."

"You mean you chose to say the necessary antidotal chant and she opted not to?"

"That's the gist of it. To look at it another way, I decided to temper my power with forethought and clarity, while she elected to use hers based on desire and passion, without concern for anyone else."

"What circumstance passed that caused her to veer out on such a selfish path?"

Helle looked away as if remembering a moment long ago. "Perhaps it didn't seem self-seeking to her at the time. Perhaps she believed she could maintain the reins of the horses that gallop wild and free in the blood of our primal Goddess ancestors." Her gaze returned to Bane. "Believe me, the impulse occurred to me as well."

"You considered letting the power loose?"

"Of course. Wouldn't you, if you were offered such? A person never thinks she will go too far. She believes she can handle what comes. Skada thought so, or maybe she just didn't care. I can't be sure."

"So she made one choice and you another."

"Yes, and it wasn't long before the power went to her head, and I mean that quite literally. I think she turned a little mad without the steadying influence of the altruistic seed atom. After a few centuries she lost perspective as well as empathy. Her own circular dreams trapped her in their web."

"Making nightmares for others."

Helle nodded. "Exactly. Which is where we find ourselves now."

Bane hesitated to ask the question. "Why wait until now to handle the situation?"

"What you're really asking is why I didn't kill the child as an infant."

Heat flared in his stomach. "Yes, I suppose I am asking that."

"Perhaps I should have." Helle gazed off into the distance. "I imprisoned Skada in a secluded location in the distant past...in ancient Norway, to be more exact. To destroy such a lineage, however, without giving the blood an opportunity to boil, seemed unnatural. Even Skada's daughter should have a chance." She stared directly into Bane's eyes. "It is one of my infrequent lapses, I suppose. Now I'm asking you to remedy the situation before it's too late."

Bane dipped his head. "Well noted."

"You'll do my bidding?"

"Aye, Goddess Helle. Consider it done." He gazed down at the cauldron into the silvery eyes and stunning countenance of Neva Jaxony.

Helle handed him a small pouch. "Inside this magical bag you will find what you need for the spell and potion. Guard it as gold."

He secured the pouch in his pocket.

She gave him an intense look, maneuvered her fingers as if to twist the air, and then turned her hands upward. On her palms rested an ancient and lethal dagger. Its obsidian handle was shaped into an intricately carved dragon's head, and the slightly curved blade glowed a faint golden green. "This is Mistilteinn, scythe of the *draugr* Prainn. Take it, warrior."

His chest thumping, he accepted the fierce weapon.

"It is forged of death magic. You understand what it is for?"

"Yes, Goddess. It is the dagger that will kill Skada's daughter, should it be necessary." He placed it into his satchel.

She nodded in approval and pointed at the symmetrical face in the cauldron. "Take full appraisal of Neva Jaxony's appearance, warrior. It is she you will have to locate among the time strands in the human world, and if the antidote fails, or time runs out, it is she you must destroy." She commanded, "Hold out your palm."

Stiffening, Bane complied, his gaze riveted on the grim visage of the powerful Goddess.

From a sash around her waist she removed another dagger, this one smaller and housed in an ornate ivory scabbard. It looked as ancient as the vast mountain ranges that cloaked the Underworld they inhabited. When she held it aloft, the torchlight glinted on the razor sharp tip. With a steady hand, she used the point of the dagger to trace an arcane symbol into the palm of his hand.

The syllables of the guttural incantation she uttered seemed to sear themselves into his soul.

His jaw clenched. Although she didn't carve out his flesh, the cut was deep enough for blood to ooze from the sides of his hand.

She released him with a mirthless smile. "This blood rune binds you to me until the task is complete. You are bound to my will."

Odin's balls. Just what he didn't need. "Why go that far, Goddess?"

"I merely hope it is far enough. There is much to do. You are charged to determine the exact time and place the girl is secreted on the human plane. Then you must cross dimensions and materialize in her location to encounter and study her, discover her predilections and intentions. Make your determination as soon as possible. Above all, you must prevent her transformation. Remember the significance of the Solstice Moon." Helle swayed a fraction as if overcome by a sudden weariness. "Go now. My fire fae will guide you safely down the labyrinthine pathways and out of my abode."

With a slight bow and a departing glance at the face of Neva Jaxony still shimmering in the cauldron, Bane departed the inner sanctum of the Goddess of the Underworld.

Chapter Two

Human World, Modern Day

Tossing down her satchel, Neva Jaxony sank cross-legged to the ground. Bending forward, she threaded her fingers through a lush patch of purple wildflowers sprouting through the carpet of pine needles. The short, slender stalks were soft and warm from the late afternoon sun. Ooh, what tiny blossoms, but ornately formed and so perfect.

A bird's stuttered caw drew her attention. Her gaze traveled up to the panorama of tall pines dancing beneath a pristine sky. She lifted her arms to the heavens and drew in a deep breath, the glorious view and crisp woodsy fragrance swelling her heart. Though she adored scented candles, nothing manufactured could stimulate the senses like the outdoors. All of the senses. If she could capture on canvas a fraction of the feeling she had right now, she'd die happy.

Some people considered nature merciless and cruel, but it soothed her soul and provided a needed solace from her otherwise studious life. A wry smile tugged at her lips. Even a starving artist and part-time teacher had to keep a roof over her head. She had papers to grade, but the work could be done tonight. She needn't worry about that right now. She had two whole hours just to laze away and paint. A pleasurable sigh escaped her, as she unzipped the satchel and removed a blank canvas, brushes, and a tub of acrylics.

Soon the rectangular white board underwent metamorphosis into whirls and splashes of cerulean, emerald, lavender, and violet. Mixing the colors with first white and then black on a paper plate, she managed an array of interesting shadings.

Acrylics were great because they were vibrant and dried fast. If she didn't like the outcome, she could paint right over the picture. Pursing her lips, she held the board at arm's length and surveyed the jumble of colors. Hmm, not too shabby. Of course the effort didn't meet her highest expectations—her paintings never did—but she liked the way the purple hues stood out in the sea of blues and greens.

When the paint settled, she swooshed the canvas back and forth in the air to hurry the drying process.

Caws shrieked above, and she looked up, startled. Two crows fought in midair, lunging toward each other and pecking. A spike of black floated down and landed on an ice blue section of the painting, sticking to its tackiness. Her heart beat faster at the strange sight. The black feather transformed the artwork, adding a different quality. No longer serene, no longer soothing. The painting now held a breath of the macabre.

She should remove the feather. She reached out her hand, but a sizzle of energy stopped her. She tilted her head and gazed at the artwork. She wasn't sure why she hesitated. Maybe she rather liked nature's unexpected gift as part of the picture after all. She bit her bottom lip. *It looks fascinating—sinister and powerful.*

She frowned. The thought sounded foreign and unlike her. Had exploring her fae heritage under the tutelage of Granny Eastwick sheered her closer to the edge? Did attraction to the darker side of life accompany such a quest? That dear soul declared her in possession of unfathomed potential. She would have to ask Granny about this.

In addition to periodic bouts of sleepwalking, she had experienced nightmares for as long as she could remember, but she hated them, shunned the eerie feelings left in their aftermath. Now it almost seemed as though her nightmares were intruding into her waking life.

A clap of thunder made her jump.

With a feeling of unease, Neva packed up the art supplies and hurried back toward her place near the campus. Good thing acrylics dried fast. She held the painting close anyway, under the threatening aspect of a gathering banner of dark clouds. The first drops of rain fell. *Damn.* She cringed at the impending image of a drenched canvas.

From out of a cluster of sycamore trees, a tall figure strode toward her.

Initially alarmed, she relaxed as he held out a dark green umbrella.

"Here, use this. Protect your work."

"Oh no, I couldn't take your umbrella."

Thunder cracked across the heavens, closer now.

"We can share until we get to the buildings." He jerked a thumb toward her canvas. "I wouldn't like to see your effort ruined." He lifted the umbrella over her just as the sky released its torrent. Together they hurried across the open area of green grass.

As they ducked under the canopy lining the main street, she turned toward him with a slight smile. "Thanks for the save." She inspected the painting and brushed away a few moist beads on the rim. "It's fine."

"May I see it?"

A nervous tremor shot up her spine at the prospect of showing someone her newest work. He had been courteous, though, and kind. She held out the painting for him to inspect.

He studied it for several moments. "Interesting."

Her cheeks heated. *Interesting*—the word people used when they didn't like an object but were too polite to hurt your feelings. She took a step sideways, turning the canvas away from him.

"It's damn good. I like the bold colors—and the feather adds an element of mystery. You have a magic touch."

Surprised, she met the full force of his gaze and was struck by the glittering gold flecks and streaks of cyan in his indigo eyes. How unusual, and striking. "Thanks. Are you...into art?"

"Not at all. But I know when I like something." He looked upward. "That was a quick Florida rainstorm." With a dexterous snap, he closed the umbrella, shook droplets of water off it, and stuck out his hand. "Bane Heughar."

She caught sight of a strange red mark in his palm. A war scar? He had the look of a soldier, muscular and fit, and the shadows behind his unusual eyes told her he had seen horrors. She placed her soft hand in his. "Neva Jaxony. Thanks again." She turned to leave.

"See you around, Neva Jaxony."

A pleasurable sensation danced over her skin at the husky way he said her name. Maybe seeing him again might be interesting and a treat to look forward to. She made her way along the sidewalk and across the green toward her little bungalow near the college. Inside she tossed her bag on the corner table and propped the canvas upright beside it. Puzzlement swept over her as she eyed the painting again with its strange transformation. It drew her in somehow, made her appreciate its macabre potential. A shiver wracked over her, leaving goose bumps on her arms. Enough of this nonsense. Tea, she needed a cup of Earl Grey, and fast, to quell the ominous feeling.

She should turn the picture around toward the wall so that it could not disturb her. She left it alone and went into the kitchen. Thanks to her recent splurge on an instant brew machine, she had hot water over a tea bag in a matter of moments. She took the mug to her tiny kitchen table and took a sip. Mmm, good tea.

A roaring noise sounded on the roof. The rain had started again. She pulled aside the yellow curtain to see outside the window. Appreciating the power of the rain and lulled by its rhythm, she relaxed and sipped her beverage. Nothing soothed her like a crisp Earl Grey.

After a few minutes she sighed and placed a hand over her heart. The unusual eerie feeling had receded, thank heaven. The rain came down in torrents now, causing the day to compress more quickly into twilight. Her free afternoon had simply flown. A sudden yawn erupted, and she stretched into it. Almost time to hit the sack. She'd better get those papers graded before she lost the energy for it.

Ugh, grading papers. She should have known she couldn't just stroll on campus and focus solely on teaching kids how to paint. Most of those "kids" were mature students, some even senior citizens. The range of ages surprised and delighted her. Art broached the universal after all.

Fetching her burgundy faux leather briefcase, she pulled out the papers. The first one she scanned brought a slight smile to her lips. Blanche Somby had titled her essay *Botticelli's Legacy for Paul Klee*. Teaching art history had turned out to be more amusing than originally anticipated. She shuffled the documents, pulling out another to review.

With a harsh gasp, her breath caught in her throat. No signature or writing appeared on the paper—just a perfect pen and ink drawing of a crow, its beak stretched wide. Neva imagined she could hear its agonized cry. Where had this come from? She studied it. The material itself gave the impression of age. It appeared to be fine parchment or old-fashioned vellum. Her hands shaking, she tossed the drawing on the table. Again, she had the sense of her nightmares materializing in real life. What the hell was happening to her?

She grabbed the phone to call her therapist. Doctor Adams specialized in treating Wytchfae, quite under the radar of normal humans, and had been helping her recover some memories of her peculiar, blank childhood. When she declared her situation an emergency, the receptionist set up an appointment right away.

Rue Adams maintained an office on the first floor of an antique house on what used to be the town's main street. Red frizzy hair helped define her as a striking, mature woman. Well-fitted tweed suits contributed to an overall image of competence and authority. To focus on anything but her own spiraling nerves, Neva admired today's ensemble in shades of dark green with sage specks throughout. The contrasting colors highlighted a ring of bluish flecks around the inner circle of the doctor's eyes.

"Sit down, Neva. Lean back and relax. I've had Hilda prepare some chamomile tea for you."

Hilda was a tiny elderly woman of European descent, spry for her advanced age. She carried in a silver tray with a beautiful gold-rimmed cup and saucer. Delicate but ornate dark pink roses decorated the set. A matching serving saucer held three cookies, or biscuits as Neva had heard Hilda call them. The design of the china reflected the busy style of the Victorian age.

Neva's fingers trembled as she accepted the drink. "Thank you, Hilda."

The servant gave a slight Old World curtsy and looked at her employer. "Anything else, madam?"

"Not now, Hilda. Thank you."

After Hilda left the room, Doctor Adams took a seat facing Neva. "You still look a bit shaken. Drink your tea and have a bite. Once you are calmer, you can tell me all about the incident that has disturbed you."

The steam rising from the cup enticed her, and she enjoyed a few sips of tea. The almond scent of the cookies stimulated her taste buds, and she bit off a morsel. "These are delicious, doctor. I've never tasted anything quite like them."

"One of Hilda's specialties. She brought many recipes with her when she came over during wartime."

Neva nodded. Another sip of tea and she began to relax a little.

"Tell me what happened."

She related the scenario of the black feather that fell on her painting and the crow picture that had appeared in her briefcase.

The doctor's expression remained calm. "Is it possible one of your students created the drawing?"

"Yes, but no one signed it, and nothing indicated it as the work of a student. It certainly wasn't part of any assignment. We're studying Klee. Plus, it was on old-fashioned material like vellum."

"Still it's possible. And the feather could be a mere coincidence as well. I know you're looking for signs. That's quite natural as you explore your

Wytchfae powers, dig into your missing childhood, and try and assimilate into a more human world as well. It's no wonder you are feeling a bit overwhelmed. You have a lot on your plate right now, Neva."

"Until a year ago I didn't even know about supernatural powers or that such things as fae existed, much less my part in the ancient bloodline. I feel perfectly inept about it all. If I hadn't met Granny Eastwick and been advised to come to you…"

The doctor smiled. "But you did come, and you will soon learn to manage all areas of your life, never fear."

Neva sighed.

"What's the sigh for?"

"Sometimes I wish I hadn't found out."

The doctor lifted a sculpted russet brow. "You would rather have lived your life as a mere human, without knowledge of your special heritage?"

She quivered at the emotion in the doctor's voice. "No, not really, it's just overwhelming sometimes."

"You've had no luck in finding information among the items in the safety deposit boxes your foster parents left you?"

"I put the boxes in the closet after I had them delivered, but I really haven't taken the time to look through them yet. They appear to contain mostly documents."

"What are you afraid of?"

A tremor shot through her. "I-I'm not sure. I keep thinking maybe I'm better off not knowing."

"We can't deal with what we don't know. Don't put it off, Neva. The sooner you understand your true heritage, the more quickly you will recover your memories and harness the power that is yours. Remember what I said in our last session—your childhood is where you will find the answers you seek. You do still seek them, don't you?"

She bit her lip. "Yes, I have to know who I really am and why I remember so little from my childhood."

"Then you must have the courage to search through the boxes."

"Yes, doctor. I'll begin tomorrow morning."

Chapter Three

A mug of Black Death coffee from her cupboard and an extra hot shower the following morning at sunrise perked Neva up at least a little. Sleep had pretty much evaded her, and strange dreams had plagued her. She had the sensation of being awake all night, though she knew she had slept in spurts. The unsettled feeling had remained with her throughout the night and continued this morning. She needed strong coffee to help her as she looked through the boxes as the doctor had urged. Might as well make a start on it.

On her birthday the bank had notified her of items left by her foster parents. It wasn't just one safety deposit box of normal size but two large ones, and one contained a key to a storage unit with more medium sized boxes. She'd had them all delivered to her house and had stored them in the closet off the kitchen. If not for the doctor's urging, she doubted she'd be in any hurry to look inside.

Inhaling deeply to bolster her nerves, she took a box and placed it on the floor by her chair. Another sip of coffee and she opened the box and pulled out some papers.

The first sheets she looked at were innocuous receipts, and eerie sensations prickled her skin while going through them. The papers could as well have belonged to a stranger, as much as the Remys had receded from her mind. Finding her unconscious on a pew of their hometown church at age seven, they took her in and offered security and support to a child who had no memory of a prior life and no clue where she came from. The Remys had died in a car crash shortly after taking her in, leaving no other relatives. She had been tossed among a variety of subsequent foster homes. Rather than waiting to age out of the system, she left the last foster home at age seventeen. Only recently had she discovered the existence of the safety deposit boxes and the other items in storage belonging to the Remys.

In the bottom of the second bundle lay a music box, black enamel with swirl designs painted in pink and green. She cooed. *Beautiful*. She opened it and recognized the tune as *Norwegian Wood*. Sometimes people kept jewelry or treasure in such a place, but nothing graced the red velvet lining. She ran her finger over it. The cloth loosened a bit, and she plucked it up. Her fingers brushed over another piece of fabric. After a quick intake of breath, she unwedged it from the box.

Made of pink satin, the fabric had been fashioned into a pocket and folded over like an envelope. Her hand trembled as she opened the flap.

A photograph! The picture showed a smiling dark haired woman holding a baby.

The breath left her. Was she the baby? Could this be her mother? Perhaps a bag or bundle containing this baby picture had been with her when the Remys found her in the church. She turned it over to see the small, rounded feminine handwriting that said, *Jewel and baby girl*. She stared at the photo for a long time and then used the camera on her phone to snap digital pictures of both sides.

She rummaged around the junk drawer in the kitchen and found an extra credit card case, one of the hard ones that helped protect against identity thieves.

She put the old photograph in the case and clicked it shut. She looked around for a cubbyhole. The picture had been well hidden for years. An urge swept over her to hide it again. She ended up climbing on a step stool and slipping it high onto the curved top of the china cabinet, where it couldn't be seen from any angle. No one would have any reason to go looking up there.

The rest of the boxes would have to wait. Her stomach rumbled with the aftermath of excitement and hunger.

Only one class this afternoon. She'd venture out for breakfast before it started. She needed to be away from her solitary self, anywhere there were people. She dreaded being alone. She couldn't bring herself to take her art supplies with her, although she usually grabbed any free time as an indulgence to produce some work. Not today. The painting with the feather and the drawing of the crow seemed to mock her as she skirted the campus and made her way toward the little café she sometimes favored. There were times when coffee and a muffin just wouldn't do.

She had come earlier than usual, and people packed the small restaurant. The voice of her favorite waitress sounded shrill in the din of conversation. "Morning, Neva. I'm afraid we're full up." Angie's cheery smile matched her bright orange uniform. She leaned close to Neva. "Table six is winding down. Hang on a couple minutes, and I'll confiscate it for you."

"Thanks, Angie."

True to her word, Angie soon led her to one of the corner tables that would only accommodate two people. "What'll it be this morning?"

"Toast and crispy bacon."

"And coffee of course."

"Yes, gallons please."

Angie laughed. "You got it, sister. Bad night?"

Neva shrugged. "It could have been better."

"They always can, honey." Angie strolled off toward the kitchen.

Neva glanced over as the front door opened. Her heart pattering, she looked away. Bane Heughar, the man who had lent her half of his umbrella, had entered the café.

Trying to appear inconspicuous, with her peripheral vision she noticed that he scanned the room. His height set him above the other diners, and his steely build reminded her of the career soldiers she had seen on the news. His gaze swept beyond her and then returned to hold for a moment. She looked up and a thrill of excitement tickled her stomach.

Recognition flickered in his eyes. Clothed in jeans and a green checked shirt open at the neck, he looked like the tastiest treat Neva had seen in a long time. Oh lord, who let him out of a warm bed? The sight of him certainly brightened up the day. Her cheeks burned at the unexpected prurient images his presence created. She wasn't used to having such an immediate physical response to a man. In fact, she had never reacted this way to a perfect stranger. With a flush of irritation at herself, she pushed the button on her smart phone and pretended to be reading.

Angie appeared with Neva's order and grinned in Bane Heughar's direction. "Good morning, Mr. Heughar." Placing Neva's toast and bacon on the table, she flipped the cup and poured coffee. "Honey, I'm about to do you a big favor. Roll with it, okay?"

She turned to the man and motioned. "Mr. Heughar, over here."

Neva's mouth fell open. A moment later the air stirred beside her, prickling her forearm with electricity. The room seemed to hum as Bane approached.

Angie continued her pleasant prattle. "We're out of tables. Have a seat here, Mr. Heughar. Neva doesn't mind, do you honey?"

Neva stiffened.

He gave her a lopsided apologetic look that sent another spurt of electricity dancing in her abdomen. "Do you mind if I sit here? I promise not to bite." His deep, resonant voice pleasured her. She found herself wanting to hear him talk.

She blinked a couple of times and cleared her throat. "Not at all." She waved a gracious hand toward the chair. "Have a seat."

His smile could melt butter. Perhaps the diner was the right place where she could put it to the test.

Angie handed the man a menu and poured coffee into his cup. She gave him a satisfied grin and tilted her head at Neva. "Bane Heughar, meet Neva Jaxony."

"Nice to see you again, Neva."

"You two know each other?"

Neva tugged at a lock of her hair. "We shared an umbrella."

"You had time to talk yet?"

His lips spread to show white teeth with the kind of sharp canines Neva had always found attractive in a man's smile. "Not yet. Maybe we will now. Thanks for saving a starving man." He extended a hand as if for an amiable shake.

Her fingers touched his for a long moment, sending a jolt up her arm.

Angie cleared her throat. "What can I get you this morning, Mr. Heughar?"

"Call me Bane. Coffee and…" He nodded toward a platter on a neighboring table. "The hotcakes look pretty good. I'll have some of those."

When Angie walked away to put in the order, Bane encouraged Neva. "Please don't mind me. Eat your breakfast while it's hot."

She slathered blackberry jam over her toast and bit into it, a little shy about munching down while he sat waiting. After the first succulent bite, she sighed in appreciation.

"Good?"

"Yes, very." She sipped coffee. "I haven't seen you around until recently. Are you new in town?"

He gave a quick nod. "Just rolled in a few days ago. You grow up around here, Neva?"

The way his tongue lingered over her name made it sound special and personal, as if only the two of them were in the room. He sure had his fair share of charisma. She set down her cup. "No, I've only been here a couple of years."

"Move here with your parents?"

Her eyes flicked downward. "No, actually I had some disagreements with my last foster parents and bugged out just before graduating high school." A slight smile played upon her lips. "I came here in a rickety stick shift that limped and lurched through every single stop light. I slept in it four months before saving enough money to rent an apartment."

Interest lit up his face. "Obviously you found a way to overcome adversity and continue school."

"Yep. I waited tables and made a good friend named Granny Eastwick. She's a dear and rather eccentric artist who creates works from found items."

His brow lifted. "Found items? You mean like seashells and old tires?"

Neva laughed. "Pretty much. From pine cones to discarded cigarette packs, she uses whatever strikes her fancy at the moment. She helped me get my life straight, finish school, and earn a little money from my own artwork."

"Granny Eastwick sounds like a remarkable lady."

"She reads tea leaves and lives a simple life. People are a little leery of her because she's different."

"She means a lot to you."

"Yes, in a way we're kindred spirits. She showed me I could make a living doing what I love best. Then I got a part-time job teaching art. It's the best of both worlds."

"Good for you. This looks like a pretty fair place to throw down some roots."

She nodded and nibbled more toast while waiting for him to elaborate. When he didn't, she couldn't resist asking a question. "Are you staying around here long?"

He shrugged. "Don't know yet. I'd like to look around a little though. Any chance you might show me the sights?"

A little thrill coursed through her blood at his request. "There's really not much to see. Are you interested in anything in particular?"

One side of his mouth quirked upward. "I heard the town boasts of a haunted house."

"Ahh, you must be referring to the old Castel house. There are tours Tuesday through Thursday. So, today at three o'clock is the last one for the week. I can show you where it is."

"I'd appreciate that. Have you taken the tour?"

"Uh, no, not really. I've been there, but I haven't officially taken the tour."

"You could come in with me and protect me from any spirits that are loose in the place. It could be fun. How about it, Neva?"

"You believe in spirits, Mr. Heughar?"

"Bane. You don't?"

She played with her fork. She had known him only a short time. It was a little too early to reveal her Wytchfae heritage. "Well, perhaps, but it's a subject I try not to dwell on."

"Surely you've noticed things beyond the ordinary."

The image of the crow's feather and the strange pen and ink drawing blared in her mind. If only he knew. Wait a minute. *Holy hell.* Was he hinting around at supernatural phenomena because fae blood ran in his veins as well? "I-I don't know. Maybe."

"We can protect each other. How about it?"

"All right. I'll go on the tour with you. I teach an art class on campus at one-thirty. Room TN-212 in the main building. It only lasts an hour."

"I'll pick you up outside your classroom at two-thirty."

Angie offered a smile as she set the piping hot cakes in front of him. Neva admired his masculine enthusiasm for digging right into his breakfast. This should prove to be an interesting day. Hanging around with Bane Heughar would be a welcome relief from crows and the doctor's orders to search her childhood for answers about her past.

True to his word, Bane waited for her outside the classroom door after the session. She eyed him. "I wondered if you'd really show up. I thought maybe you'd find something more interesting to do than ghost hunting."

"Stand up a beautiful woman? Not a chance. I'm a man of my word. Good class?"

She nodded and flung her satchel over her shoulder. She'd do her level best to enjoy the day— not a date—and put from her mind any uneasy feelings and the blank wall of her early years.

The old Castel house stood a few short blocks from campus. She liked living in a place with all the good stuff clumped nearby. Although the inevitable fast food joints and shops had sprung up near the campus, they tended to be over toward the west. On this side, the old main street, now a back street, on the east side of campus, things remained more as they were fifty years ago. There were signs of change, though, and Neva mourned the loss of several of the antique homes that had once stood along the street.

"The Castel house is that two story just ahead."

He surveyed the old structure. "Tell me about it."

"Well, the historical society is working toward getting it placed on the National Register of Historic Places."

"Interesting colors."

She laughed. "Yeah, it's funny the taste of some people."

"I can go for the mint green of the bottom story, but the top is a little much."

"What, you're not partial to confection pink?"

He chuckled. "I can live without it."

"I'm rather fond of the way it looks. Always makes me think of cotton candy."

He reached out to rub a thumb across the rough stucco that had been slathered over the original wood at some point, giving the impression of a stone mansion. "I wonder what the ghost thinks about the changes."

"Ghosts," Neva corrected. "There are reported to be several."

Chapter Four

A middle-aged woman met Neva and Bane at the door of the old Castel house. Neva recognized her from the historical society meetings she sometimes attended. "Hello, Neva, nice to see you." Her gaze traveled over Bane, up and down, and a wide grin split her face. She obviously enjoyed what she saw.

Neva took the lead. "Marcia Simmons, this is Bane Heughar. He's interested in the Castel ghosts."

"Ahh, very nice to meet you, Bane. Come right in and join the others. Please sign the book, and the tour will begin shortly. Don't forget to fill out all the information, including your phone number." She winked at Bane.

They broke away from their perusal of old paintings and knick-knacks as the tour started.

Midway through the tour they were led into an upstairs study. While Bane and the others listened to Marcia tell about the original Castel family from a century past and the ghosts that inhabited the house, which Neva had heard several times at historical meetings, her attention wandered to an array of tall bookshelves. Tiptoeing to the collection, she traced a finger over one of the ornate old books. Glancing at Marcia, who had her interest riveted on Bane and didn't pay her the slightest bit of attention, Neva pulled the volume off the shelf. Its weight nearly bent her double, and she hefted it onto the nearby table.

She opened the book. The decorative gold-rimmed pages with the Old English-style font mesmerized her. The book entitled *Myths of the World* was authored by a Mrs. Eunice Uttersen. Neva marveled at the unique drawings and colorful illustrations. She squeezed her eyes shut and placed fingertips at her temples. *Let's see what my special message is for today.* As she sometimes did to receive divinatory information, Neva turned to a random page toward the end of the book. The face of a beautiful woman stared back at her. With pale blonde hair and blue grey eyes, the woman stood in the middle of a snowy landscape. *The Snow Queen*. It had always been one of her favorite stories. This particular version stemmed from Norway.

How wonderful it would be to visit there. Neva allowed her mind to wander a bit with the possibility of traveling the world. Norway would definitely be one of the places on her journey. With its breathtaking scenery what could be more scintillating?

As she stared into the snowy landscape depicted on the page, she found herself drifting, as though she were having an out-of-body experience. The letters on the page shimmered, shifted, and rearranged themselves. A moment later they had formed the outline of a crow, one with coal black feathers. Not only that, but the gold leaf had spelled out a name. *Neva.*

She gasped and slammed the book closed.

Bane glanced over and then came toward her. "What is it? You look like you've seen a ghost."

"N-nothing. Just a picture in this old book."

"Show me."

Fearing the crow and her spelled out name would still be there, she opened it to the page of *The Snow Queen* that she had been looking at. It now appeared normal.

He touched one of the illustrations. "Ahh, this lady is a treacherous creature." His gaze swept to hers, and heat touched her cheeks at his intense scrutiny.

She shrugged. "Yes, some people think so. I love her story though. She had great power, and sometimes it's hard for others to be comfortable in the presence of a strong woman."

"So you think people misunderstood her?"

"Oh, you've read the story too?" Neva wrinkled her nose. "Possibly. Don't you?"

"I doubt it. She had it in pretty bad for that poor boy she kidnapped. She did a good job of torturing the kid."

"I think she loved him and wanted to keep him nearby."

His brow lifted. "Is that how you see it?"

"How do *you* summarize the story?"

"Sorceress craves, sorceress carves, sorceress caves."

"Caves? As in gives in? Caves in to what?"

He shrugged. "The power of evil perhaps."

Uneasy, Neva smiled and placed the book back on the shelf. "Succinctly put. Shall we rejoin the others?"

The remainder of the tour maintained a light tone. Afterward, when Bane escorted her back to the college, where she had to pick up the late mail, he stopped at the entrance and took her hand in his. "Like to see a movie with me tonight?"

His gentle touch caused a flutter in her stomach. She had the impulse to say yes, if just to hang around him a little more. Afraid to make a pure fool out of herself over the man, she declined. "I'm a little tired, and I have papers to grade before morning."

"How about tomorrow evening then? If not a movie, maybe we can grab a meal—or…you name the activity."

"How long did you say you're in town?"

His eyes twinkled. "I didn't, but I'm finding more reason to hang around every minute."

Neva laughed. "I'd enjoy a meal. We have to eat. Same diner at six o'clock, or would you prefer a fancier place?"

"The diner suits me. What about you?"

"It suits me too. They serve breakfast all day. See you there."

* * * *

As he walked away from Neva, Bane clenched his jaw. He had to wonder again why the Goddess of the Underworld had chosen him for the job of watching the Wytchfae for signs of transformation, despite the acclaim of being named Odin's warrior. In his mind, medals didn't make the man. She said she needed his subtlety as well as his ruthlessness. Yes, he had worked as a soldier and killed when he had to, but subtlety and subterfuge were not his strong suits. Neva's beauty took his breath away. She exuded qualities more unworldly than the women he usually went for. Yet, he found himself drawn to her ethereal looks. Plus, the more time he spent with her, the more he liked her.

The Goddess Helle had ordered him to observe Neva and watch her for signs of possession by dark forces that could lead to transformation into a demoness. Thank Odin she seemed to like him well enough to let him hang around. Otherwise, he'd be constantly leering at her from the shadows, as he did now. He couldn't let her out of his sight for long. The Goddess Helle depended on him.

The many Underworld domains did so as well. No one knew what revenge the demoness daughter of Skada would seek on those who had imprisoned her mother and squelched her powers. She posed a danger for everyone concerned.

A sudden pain seared through his hand, eliciting a groan. The damnable blood rune of the Goddess Helle reminded him time was short. The solstice approached and, before that, the metaphysical trigger of the Solstice Moon when Neva could turn dark. He squeezed his hand as hard as he could, crushing off the pain.

He shook his head, ignoring the curious looks of two or three strangers who passed his lookout spot. Stay focused on the mission. He may appreciate the woman Neva, but he would dispatch evil without hesitation. Working to contain the hideous vampiric Grims in the Underworld had accustomed him to swift objective action. He had to be ready to kill Neva before she turned into a demoness. If he failed in his mission, she might well transform into that most loathsome of undead creatures, a *draugr*. He wouldn't wish that on his worst enemy.

Much less a stunning woman like Neva.

* * * *

Neva heaved a sigh as she unlocked the door to her bungalow and stepped inside. Away from Bane's charming presence, she fell into a brooding, morose state. She cursed the day she had left the most recent foster home. At that time her seventeen-year-old emotions could no longer stand the restrictions put on her by her foster mother and the vile names heaped at her because of her passion for artwork and desire to be alone. It wasn't that she didn't like people. She did. But she needed alone time too, a necessity her social butterfly of a foster mother hadn't understood. Nor did her foster mother comprehend her passion for painting. "You can't make a living as an artist, Neva. Don't be ridiculous. If you'd just apply yourself to your schoolwork, you could be anything you want to—a lawyer, a doctor, a worthwhile career instead of random sketches and unsightly paint on your hands and clothes all the time. La, the washing of your clothes. It costs at least double what it should in detergent."

To her young aspiring mind, the criticism didn't make sense. If she could be anything she wanted, why couldn't she be an artist? She figured out it was because the profession, or hobby as her foster mother described it, lacked the necessary and coveted prestige. But she longed to paint, along with traveling and seeing the world, her other passion. Not that she didn't love Florida, with its eternal summer, beaches, and deep forest wildflowers—so delicate and lovely to paint. But she also wanted to see Greece, Egypt, Ireland, Scotland, Norway—all the historic and culturally rich places she dreamed about.

Her dreams were another thing her foster mother objected to. Neva frightened her mother by sometimes waking in the night screaming, and by the habit she had of sleepwalking, which happened once or twice a week. It unraveled her too, and she had never revealed most of the dreams she had, so vivid, so terrifying. Even when her mother sent her to see a psychologist because of her unruly dreams and sleepwalking, she didn't reveal all of the true facts to the therapist. She held on to the scariest parts, where she saw blood, murder, and other vile unmentionable acts.

The psychologist told her parents she had been scarred in some way in early childhood and the dreams and sleepwalking were a result of that. Neva couldn't disagree with the explanation, since she couldn't remember anything at all before the age of seven. It was as if she had woken up one morning and lived, whereas she already had seven years under her belt. She entered school late because of her age and fell a year behind her class, another factor in her sensitivity toward schoolwork, teachers, and some of her bright or noisy and ultra-assertive fellow students. She always perceived herself as different, maybe even a little inferior. She might as well be an alien baby left on an earthling's doorstep. Not that she believed in such things. But the loneliness of her heart whispered her otherness.

Added to that, her foster father had begun to look at her with a lecherous gleam in his eyes. His gaze would linger on her breasts a few seconds too long. It really creeped her out. His changed behavior made her feel unclean and no longer comfortable in hugging him, not that he'd ever been an especially affectionate father figure. Once not long before she left home for good, he asked her if she was still a virgin. She had just stared at him with a blank feeling in her heart. "Have you been with a boy, Neva?"

"N-no."

He had come closer to her then, and she backed up a step. "Do you like older men then?"

"No, I don't. Leave me alone. That's disgusting."

At that, he had let her be, but she went over and over the conversation in her mind. If it hadn't been for the incident, she probably wouldn't have run away from those latest foster parents, despite her differences with them. But his demeanor and pointed questions had freaked her out to the point where she couldn't stay in the same house. She had probably overreacted and should have talked to someone about it. But she just couldn't discuss it, not even with Aubyn, her closest friend in school.

Before completing high school, she packed her meager belongings in a duffel bag with her few art supplies, pocketed the money she had saved from working after school in the local fast food joint, and skedaddled.

Her first piece of good fortune came when she ended up at this spot on Florida's west coast. Not the wave crested beaches of the east coast, rather a gentler, more rural location where she could work, paint, and keep to herself. Just the way she liked it. Her second piece of good luck appeared in the form of her friend Granny Eastwick. Not only was Granny an artist, but also a Wytchfae. She became Neva's mentor.

At the first mention of her otherworldly powers, a deep light had shone in Granny Eastwick's eyes. "Some call me a witch because I know things."

Neva had looked at her, startled. At that time she hadn't heard of real witches or fae. "Are you a witch?" She had been halfway kidding.

To her surprise, Granny Eastwick had nodded. "I am a Wytchfae. My mother always said so, and events have proven it. She birthed me as the seventh of seven daughters, as did her mother before her. Have you heard of the fae, Neva?"

"The fae, as in fairies?"

"Yes, but not the kind in your children's fairy tales. The variety that really do exist, just a touch away from our sight. Some visit our worlds. I've seen them. As well, my old mother always held that our family had fae blood in us."

Neva didn't know what to say, but it fascinated her. "I wish I had fae blood."

"Mebbe you do."

"Why do you say that?"

"Because of your temperament and how skilled you are with your paints and what not. I wouldn't be surprised. After all, you said you don't remember much about your early childhood."

After the conversation with Granny Eastwick, all Neva could think about involved fae blood and whether she had it in her. In one way she desperately wanted it to be true. It would explain her odd out of touch feeling, as well as perhaps the horrible nightmares. However, if such blood caused the nightmares, rather than early childhood trauma as the psychologist had maintained, then maybe she didn't want to know about any fae heritage. Uncertainty shook her. Desire and curiosity won out though, and she found herself asking Granny Eastwick an endless supply of questions. She wanted to learn about being the seventh daughter born with a veil over her face and anything else she could think of about the old woman's cultural history.

She spent some happy times with her elder friend. The wildflowers that grew in the forest near Granny Eastwick's house delighted her. She watched other people walk right by them, and stomp on them without a care in the world, but she would squat in the grass and inspect them. She had bought a smart phone with money she had saved and used its camera to take pictures of the tiny buds.

Granny Eastwick had seemed impressed by her choices. "What is it about the little buggers that enthrall you so?"

"Wildflowers don't have the big showy blooms of store bought roses and gardenias. The blossoms are small, their scent subtle. Yet they are more appealing to my senses than any store bought or cultivated plant." Their delicate nature brought out her protective instincts. They were wild and they awakened some kind of feelings and energies within her that longed to come forth. And emerge they did, on her drawing pad and especially on her canvas. From purple wild day flowers with their bright yellow centers to the splotches of yellow bonnets to the tall magenta spikes of blazing stars—all made their way onto Neva's canvas.

Then she began to paint them with wings, as little fairies, after her inspirational conversations with Granny Eastwick. Flower fairies. She imagined they were wild flowers in the human dimension and fae beings in the otherworldly dimension Granny Eastwick always talked about. She also began traveling on the weekends with Granny Eastwick while the old woman sold her art pieces along the roadside. "Bring some of your paintings with you, child. They'll sell. Take my word for it."

And they did, to Neva's astonishment. Having no clue what prices to ask for her paintings, she took her cue from Granny Eastwick. That soul maintained people would pay for artwork if it appealed enough to their senses, but an artist had to entice the buyers on the spur of the moment and not let them have time to think about it. She told Neva an artist should go where the people are. Hence, selling along the roadside in a casual manner trumped hanging around a gallery where people purposefully sought out art. The goal seemed to become part of ordinary humanity instead of being stuck in an artists' conclave. What a common sense philosophy. It worked for Granny Eastwick, who had to pick up fewer cans to make money as time went by, because her art pieces sold pretty well and she didn't need a great deal of money to live. She didn't splurge on anything and didn't even own a television.

Neva finished school and obtained a part-time job teaching art. Despite her continuing gory nightmares and occasional bout of sleepwalking, she bore it all pretty well until a crow feather marred her painting and a black pen and ink drawing materialized in her briefcase. Feeling out of control and beset by a sense of foreboding, her burgeoning world turned topsy-turvy.

Chapter Five

Holy hell. How had she come to be atop a college dorm at night in her thigh length sleep shirt and with no shoes? She bit back a sharp gasp. With her bare feet clamped to the cold stone, Neva peered down in shock at the toy like cars in the dim parking lot below. The pavement seemed to beckon her downward. Averting her eyes, she swayed on the ledge. Fear knotted her stomach into a tight ball of ice. Afraid of toppling off, she clenched her fists to avoid giving into a black pit of panic. She remembered turning over onto her stomach in bed and closing her eyes. How had she come to be here? She used peripheral vision to scan her location. Darkness and settling mist prevented her from seeing well.

Quivering began at her toes and rushed up to a juddering crescendo in her heart as her heels curved over the narrow parapet. She tried to look down without turning her head, afraid the slightest wobble would send her hurling downward. There had to be a floor just behind her. She couldn't tell for sure. Dare she simply step backward? She froze into immobility, her nerves shattered. In a few seconds she would have to take a chance or the trembles would send her over the edge anyway.

Voices entered her consciousness, as if a group of people came closer.

"Hey, what is that chick doing out on the wall?"

"Get down from there, you crazy bitch! Hey, let me snap a picture. It will go viral for sure."

"Hush, Wyatt," urged a female voice. "You'll make her jump."

"Well, let her do a damn swan dive. We're only five stories up. She'll probably just break a leg."

"Oh, for God's sake, shut the hell up. I knew you had too much tequila."

Neva squeezed her trembling hands tighter, digging the nails into her palms. Why couldn't she move? She seemed frozen stiff. Could she possibly be home asleep and dreaming? *Oh, my goddess, what's wrong with me?*

"Step back, folks." The voice sounded deep and authoritative. It made her want to listen to it instead of the other voices and the buzzing in her ears. Warm arms scooped her off the ledge, easing her backward onto a balcony. "Just relax. I've got you."

Her legs gave way, and she sank against a rock hard chest.

The man who had intervened in her crazy escapade lifted her into his arms. "There's nothing else to see, folks. Get inside and sleep it off. I'll take care of her."

A female voice lilted. "Why, it's Ms. Jaxony! I'm in her art class. What's she doing out here?"

The reassuring masculine voice sounded again, the one that made her feel safe. "Sleepwalking, I imagine. Go inside. Your teacher may need medical attention. Don't worry. I'll make sure she's all right."

Strong arms secured her, and her cheek encountered a muscular shoulder that provided a sensation of comfort. Fogginess scrambled her brain. "Bane, is that you? Wh-what's happening?"

"Shh, just relax and let me get you out of here."

She burrowed her face against his neck to avoid having to meet anyone's eyes and to drown out the sounds of murmuring and exclamations from the small group of onlookers.

Her head throbbed at the jostling as they maneuvered down the steps. She should stay awake, but doing so seemed too much trouble, and she longed to escape the horror of the last few minutes. Bane would take care of her. He had said so. She closed her eyes.

She opened them again when a spiky plant brushed against her foot, an azalea bush—one of a row. Neva became aware Bane still carried her. She took stock of her surroundings. They had passed the path to her house. "W-where are you taking me?"

"To an emergency clinic."

She stiffened. "No, please. I'm fine now."

"Do you remember where you were?"

Despair thudded in her breast as she pictured herself standing on the stone parapet at the college. She swallowed to eradicate the feeling of shame and powerlessness. "Yes, but I want to go home." She struggled in his arms. "Put me down."

With a gentle touch, he set her feet on the sidewalk, maintaining hold of her waist. Her knees buckled, and he swept her back up into his arms. "You need a doctor."

"I'm just a little woozy, not injured or out of my mind. Take me home—please."

As he turned around and started in the general direction of her house, a sense of unquiet swept over her. How did he know which way to go? In response, her heart pattered a puzzled tattoo. He had helped her, rescued her really, but what did she know about this man? That he was a delectable hunk of male, yes. That he was good company and solicitous of her well-being, true. Yet she sensed curious mysteries and hidden depths in Bane, more so than appearances indicated. She steeled herself to keep up her guard around him.

At the door to her bungalow, he released her from his arms. He set her on the open stoop, and she dug under the mat for the front door key and, inserting it, turned the doorknob. She faced him. "Thank you, Bane. I'll be fine now. See you tomorrow. Good night."

He reached past her to push the door the rest of the way open. "Ordinarily I wouldn't be so thick skinned as to ignore a beautiful woman's brush off. Not this time. You are in no condition to be alone right now. I'm coming in until I know you're okay."

His demeanor brooked no argument, and fatigue prevented her from forcibly tossing him out. With a degree of meekness, she preceded him into the house and on into the kitchen.

On the way he grabbed an afghan from the couch.

She lowered a box of Earl Grey from the cupboard and turned on the instant brew machine to heat.

"Sit down. I'll do that." He tucked the coverlet around her shoulders.

She pulled it to her, shivering. How had she gotten so cold?

As he rummaged on the shelves and removed two mugs, surprise crept over her at how natural he appeared as he looked after her. After inserting tea bags into the cups, he positioned one under the brew spout, pushed a button, and continued opening cupboards.

"What are you searching for?"

"Whiskey. Brandy. You need a stiffener."

She sighed. A drink would hit the spot. "Bottom right."

He deposited the liquor on the table. The brew machine blinked ready. He set a cup of tea in front of her and repeated his actions with the brew machine and his own cup. Then he sat down across from her. "How are you feeling?"

"Better." She quailed at offering any explanations of her behavior. After all, what could she say? The silence stretched out as the tea seeped. His presence both disconcerted and soothed her at the same time. She contented herself with studying the shape and appearance of his hands. Their masculinity and obvious strength mesmerized her. She itched to draw their square shape, with the sexy prominent veins that gave her a giddy hitch in her breath. What a time to have such an irrelevant urge.

A few moments later he removed the tea bags and splashed a hefty shot of whiskey into each cup.

Sipping, she sighed with pleasure as the hot toddy livened up her blood flow. "Truly I'm much better now. You can feel free to leave. I'll be all right."

He set down his cup. "If you are feeling better, then explain what the hell you were doing out there about to sail off a ledge."

Flustered, she shook her head. "I had no intention of jumping."

"It sure looked like it."

"N-no."

"Then what were you doing?"

She inhaled deeply, seeking the comfort of a deep belly breath. She squeezed the cup between her hands. "To be honest, I don't have a clue. I woke up on the damn ledge. I must have been sleepwalking."

"Is that a usual occurrence?"

"What do you mean?"

"Do you have a habit of sleepwalking?"

"S-sometimes. Nothing like this though."

The pronouncement appeared to unsettle him, and he spent a few moments inspecting the inside of his cup. "You need to see a doctor. Find out about it."

"You mean a head doctor."

"Either way, a psychiatrist, psychologist, or a plain ole GP."

Bane's suggestion that she should see a psychologist cut her too close for comfort. She pursed her lips. "It just so happens I see a psychologist regularly." When he appeared startled, she hurried to explain. "Not for anything horrible I've done. For recurring nightmares and to try and help me recover my memory. I can't remember anything from my early childhood."

His look of interest reminded her she had vowed not to trust him. She bit her lip. "Bane, how did it happen you were at the right place at the right time tonight?"

His jaw clenched. "I took a late night walk and heard the shouts."

A likely story. It didn't ring true. She frowned. "When I insisted on coming home, how did you know where to bring me?"

He met her eyes. "You told me. Don't you remember?"

It was possible. She had been incredibly groggy. She shook her head.

"You were out of it. That's not unusual after what you went through. So you'll call your doctor?"

She covered a yawn. The shot of whiskey had begun to perform its magic. "First thing tomorrow."

He nodded and stood up. "Good. Now you need to be in bed. I'll bunk on the couch and make sure you don't take any more strolls tonight."

That woke her up. Her eyes widened. "No way."

"I practically saved your life. You won't give me a bed for the night?"

She blinked at him. "You don't have a place to stay?"

"Nope. Take pity, will you?"

"What would you have done if you hadn't encountered me on the ledge?"

He shrugged. "Found a park bench I suppose."

She sucked in a deep breath. "Okay then." She stood up. "There are pillows and coverings in the hall closet. I'll get them for you."

He moved a step closer.

She still basked in the sensations his warm hard body had stirred within her as he carried her down the darkened pathway.

His finger lifted her chin. "I'll take care of it. Go to bed, all right?"

"I probably will eventually, but to be honest, I'm just a little leery of doing so right now. Would you stay up and talk to me for a while?"

He nodded. "It's natural. I wouldn't want to fall asleep after such a nightmarish escapade either. Tell you what. I'm about as harmless as a gnat. You know that, right?"

She gave him a wry look. "I doubt that's true."

"We'll sit here on the couch and talk until dawn if you want to. On the other hand, if you get sleepy, just lean back and let the *ZZ*'s take over. I'll watch over you. Agreed?"

She couldn't help the sigh of relief that escaped her lips. With a slow smile, she flicked on the radio, sank down by him on the couch, and pulled a square pillow to her stomach. She would take him up on his offer, but weariness notwithstanding, she vowed to be wide awake for the first flicker of sunrise. No way would she risk another incident like the one earlier tonight. Her attention again became riveted on the noticeable blue veins of his muscular hands. They were sexier than hell. Despite the horror of the sleepwalking incident, with Bane lounging beside her, the night had certainly perked right up.

Chapter Six

Bane stayed true to his word of keeping watch and, regardless of her fatigue, Neva kept her promise to herself to stay awake. When daylight filtered through the windowpane, she set about making batches of strong coffee. When she handed him a mug of the steaming brew, he blew on it and reminded her she had promised to see a doctor. Afterward, he left to "check on some things." Was the scar in his hand acting up? It looked redder than usual, and he had grimaced and clenched his hand a few times over coffee.

As it happened, Doctor Adams had left town for the rest of the week. A trickle of guilt imbedded itself in Neva's conscience, but she also gave a sigh of relief at not having to be told she needed medication or worse. She'd go and pick Granny Eastwick's brain instead. Maybe that fine old soul could provide some insight into all this craziness.

She picked up her cell phone to call Granny Eastwick. Then she put it back down on the table. She'd go over there instead.

Granny Eastwick's cottage stood near a little copse of wooded area on the outskirts of town and within easy walking distance of campus and Neva's place. When Neva knocked, Granny Eastwick answered the door in a bathrobe, her salt and pepper hair done up in a thin towel. "Why, Neva, I'm glad to see you. Did I forget an appointment?"

"No, I-I need to talk to you if you don't mind."

"Of course I don't mind." She opened the door wide and waved her in. "Come sit down in the kitchen, dearie. What's troubling you?"

Neva told her about the feather marring her painting and the strange drawing of the crow that had materialized among her papers. Removing the painting and drawing from the cloth bag on her shoulder, she placed them on the table for Granny Eastwick to examine.

The older woman bent over them, her expression serious. "And you've no idea how the pen and ink of the crow got into your briefcase?"

Neva shook her head.

"Neva, this is important. Have you experienced any missing time?"

Neva's eyes widened and a surge of energy swirled in her stomach. "Yes. Oh, Granny Eastwick, I'm in terrible trouble." She told her about the sleepwalking incident and standing on the edge of the ledge.

Granny Eastwick gasped, and horror contorted her features. "How did you keep from falling, Neva?"

"A man I recently became acquainted with happened to be walking by and heard the commotion." Disbelief rang in her words.

"He told you that?"

"Yes."

"You don't believe him, do you?"

Neva wrung her hands together in anguish. "No. Oh, I don't know. It seems so improbable."

"I mentioned when you started along the Wytchfae path, Neva, that I feel you have power you aren't aware of. It needs to be understood and tamed. I can't say for certain if what has been happening to you is a result of your natural exploration or if you are a target in some way. In other words, is this energy coming from inside you or is an outside force directing the show?"

Bile rose in her throat. "Outside force? What do you mean?"

"To be honest I get the sense that the strange events are not your doing, and are not merely incidental magic. Your fate is at hand. A great power is calling you."

"Do you think the man Bane Heughar is involved?"

"His energy may be cloaked. The only sense I get about him is that he is more than he seems."

"That's enough reason to avoid him."

"Mebbe. Let's read the leaves."

Granny Eastwick made tea for Neva, chanted a few words, poured out the liquid, and gazed, motionless, at the residue.

Her eyes glazed over.

Neva recognized the signs of trance. She sat spellbound, waiting.

Granny Eastwick's voice echoed as if it came from a deep hollow well. "The babe must take the fated reins. *She* calls to her. *He* comes for her."

Granny Eastwick blinked several times and released a muffled groan.

Neva gave a sigh of relief when her mentor's eyes once again became clear and controlled. "Fate calls to you and there is danger. You must look to your childhood. Therein will you find answers." Her brow wrinkled with worry. "Trust no one, not even yourself. Dark powers are afoot. You must be vigilant. I have faith in you. Make use of Reiki and your pendulum. It's a providential tool for you. Take care, child. Whatever you do, take care."

As she left Granny Eastwick's her cell phone jangled, and the name of her supervisor at the college appeared. Puzzled, she took the call. "Hello?"

The sandpapery voice of Dean Little's secretary Eva came over the phone. The usually friendly woman sounded all business. "Neva, the Dean would like to see you in his office."

"Uh, sure. You mean now?"

"Yes, as soon as possible. How long will it take you to get here?"

"Just a few minutes. What's wrong, Eva?"

"I'm not free to discuss the matter. The Dean will explain." The phone went silent.

With a sinking feeling in the pit of her stomach, Neva hurried to the Dean's office. He himself awaited her at the door and ushered her to a chair. Although he tended to be a serious man, she had never seen his expression so grim. Swallowing over the lump in her throat, she waited for him to tell her what he wanted.

He rounded his desk and lowered himself into a cushioned, walnut colored leather chair. His hands steepled. "Neva, it has come to my attention that you caused quite a disturbance last night outside one of the dormitories."

Her heart sank. He had heard about the incident on the ledge. "Dean Little, I'm sorry for that, truly."

With a flourish he turned his desktop monitor around for her to view. It looked like one of the popular social media sites.

Her mouth fell open as a gasp escaped her lips. There on the screen big as life she stood on the ledge. In her black nightshirt, she looked like a vulture.

He clicked the mouse.

The next picture showed her up in the arms of Bane Heughar, her bare legs draped over his arm. Her tousled hair bunched up in disarray, and her face looked ashen.

"You're fortunate the police weren't called, Neva. As it is, at least one person on the board is calling for your resignation, and I suspect the others will be calling me any moment. Were you drunk or what's the story?"

"Of course not. I-I was sleepwalking. I woke up standing on that ledge."

His expression didn't change. "This is a type of publicity the college can't afford, Neva. If what you say is true, if you have a medical condition, then you need to get it seen to. I'm placing you on administrative leave as of now. Eva will send you the paperwork for your doctor to fill out, and at that time the leave will become medical."

"B-but, Dean Little, what about my classes?"

His phone buzzed. He pushed a button and spoke into the machine. "Not now, Eva. Tell him I'm in a meeting and will call him back shortly." He looked at Neva. "That was another board member. I told you the rest would be calling. Neva, I have no choice. We'll find a substitute to fill in the rest of the semester. Good luck getting the help you need. Once you're medically cleared, give me a call and we'll see." He stood up, effectively dismissing her.

Not knowing what else to do, Neva rose as well. As she left the office, the formerly jocund Eva failed to meet her eyes.

Neva had hoped she might hear from Bane, but the silence on that front deafened her. Determined to find out more information about her past, she vowed to scour through the remaining boxes that night. She had a strange feeling the baby in the photo with the dark haired woman might be her, although she had no real reason to think so, except that it had been hidden. There had to be another hint that would point her to the truth of her past, a discovery to trigger the memories she desperately needed.

Most of what she found could be categorized as interesting but not pertinent to her quest. Then came the jackpot. Wedged between the pages of a ledger was an old journal. Right away she sensed it might be significant. With trembling fingers she opened it to see the name Jewel Orsen written in rounded lettering. A thrill shot through her. Beneath the name were the words *My Diary* and a date. A quick calculation revealed the woman had been the age of twenty-two about seven years before Neva turned up in that church.

Was Jewel her mother? Doubt simmered low in her abdomen. How did she get the name Neva Jaxony then?

Her heart thumping in her chest, she poured over the writings, most of which revolved around a young man named David that Jewel had just met. They fell in love and got married with only a few friends in attendance. Neither had family so it seemed, or at least family who cared. Jewel at least longed for a child, but one did not seem to be forthcoming.

A child of our own. I know we shall have one, despite what the doctors say. David thinks I am delusional, no matter how hard he denies it and tries to be supportive.

Then another entry shed more light.

She came today, the blonde lady who heard my yearning and has been invading my dreams. She said she dwells in the old North Land—in an onyx cavern near the edge of the Troll's Path. She has traveled across time and space to fulfill my dream of a child. She is bringing a baby to David and me, and we are to call the babe Neva Jaxony. The nameless lady charges me to keep the baby safe from her enemies. When I asked how a baby could have enemies, the lady's face became so sorrowful that I feared for her collapse. She said the enemies were hers and they would not let her rest, nor would they allow her child to live. Can you imagine—the poor babe? I cannot tell David this, as it would be further evidence of my instability.

Then later the entries talked about Neva.

The baby is here—our little Neva. David doesn't understand, but he keeps silent for my sake. I see him looking at her strangely, as if she is a changeling, a fairy child. She may well be, but I know he will grow to love her. She has the sweetest smile. She is my little angel.

There were more pages describing little Neva's toddling ways and then—nothing. What had happened to her foster parents? Did they die like the Remys after them? They must have done so. Although she tried, she could not remember anything before she woke up in that church, orphaned.

Squeezing her eyes shut, Neva rose from the chair. What should she do? Not only was she from another place, but also another time. Had Jewel written the truth, or had she fabricated the story out of mental anguish?

Her hands clenched as she attempted to take it all in. It shouldn't be such a shock. She understood from Granny Eastwick that the fae folk and the occasional Wytchfae enjoyed time travel along the same vein as humans took an annual vacation. It had simply never occurred to her…that she…not in a million years had she considered she might not be from this time.

She swallowed, feeling a bit nauseous. She would research this Troll's Path where the blonde woman came from and then perhaps get on a plane. She had no job to worry about, and she didn't know if she could bear to stay so near the college right now. Plus, she needed to find out what was happening to her. The answers lay in her past. Both Doctor Adams and Granny Eastwick had said so. Her bones and blood told her the truth of it.

Now that she had learned of the onyx cavern in the North Land, the place called to her. The feeling simulated an unquenchable thirst, one she couldn't ignore. Surely such a place as an onyx cavern stood as a code of some sort, or as an illusion or a metaphor.

But what if the place really existed? What if that cavern, a fae stronghold to be sure, held the secrets of her birth? She clucked her tongue against the roof of her mouth. Had crazy taken over?

She stiffened her spine. Despite the events she couldn't explain, her sanity remained intact. Information about her birthright existed near a place called the Troll's Path.

Flinging open her tablet, her fingers flew over the keyboard in search of such a location.

Holy hell. There it was. Trollstigen, Norway. The Troll's Path. The pulse hammered in her throat.

Selecting a map, she ran a forefinger over the words on the screen. She scanned the surrounding villages.

She pushed the monitor to a prone position. Removing her crystal pendulum from her pocket, she held its long string above the screen with her forefinger and thumb. "Goddess, hear my plea. I seek my birthplace near the Troll's Path in the North Land." She closed her eyes. "Guide me, oh ancient one." Electricity pulsated in her fingers, as the pendulum began to move. She kept her eyes shut, freeing her mind, and couldn't tell if the divination tool moved in a circle or swung back and forth. The mysterious and magical power of the Goddess assisted her. After a few moments, the pendulum rested. Opening her eyes in anticipation, Neva followed the tip of the crystal down to the map where it pointed. A village called Valldal.

Dread thudded in her heart, along with anticipation. What would she find there? Nothing, or everything?

Chapter Seven

Despite the approach of solstice, summer weather had not yet come to Norway. At least nothing like the usual temperatures of Central Florida. Neva jerked the hood over her ears and pulled the coat tighter around her to keep out some of the chill. Luckily, a store clerk had been helpful in outfitting her with the proper clothing and boots so that she wouldn't freeze as she explored the area.

The spectacular views, everywhere she cast her eyes, quite simply took her breath away. Norway's splendor exceeded any landscape she had ever seen. With the grandeur of such immense mountains, no wonder the gods were reported to still vacation along their peaks.

When her plane had first landed, she had rented a car and taken a room in one of the big hotels. Tomorrow she planned to take the car and then the ferry and head toward the village of Valldal near the location of Trollstigen, the Troll's Path. Legend considered the region an ancient holy place where the old gods lived and evil creatures roamed in the dead of night. Throwing caution to the wind, she steeled her will to rely on her intuition and the innate sixth sense of her fae powers to lead her to the right spot. Her fingers massaged the crystal pendulum in her coat pocket. Granny Eastwick had faith in her abilities. She would too.

Shivering, she gritted her teeth. What a weather wuss. During this short walk on the hotel grounds, she could swear her skin now held a blue tinge. The cold here seeped through her clothing and penetrated her skin like needles. Oh great, now the wind had picked up. Swirls began to bite into her bones. Evening approached. Although impatience shredded her nerves, the original plan won out. She'd hang out nice and cozy in the hotel tonight with a relaxing glass of wine—or two—and set off to the village tomorrow.

As she reentered the double doors of the hotel in a hurry to get warm, she ran headlong into a tall figure. "Sorry, I..." Her hand flew to her chest.

"Bane, w-what in hell are you doing here? Are you following me?"

His neck muscles corded, and she backed up a step.

"Are you running away from me, Neva?"

She bit her lip.

Then he quirked a smile, the one she had become familiar with over the past several days.

"Truth is, a buddy wired me some money he owed me, and it burnt a hole in my pocket. By the way, thanks for the message you left for me with Angie canceling our dinner date. When she told me about your trip, I decided to visit this part of the world too. I hoped we could continue getting to know one another."

Her stomach quivered, and she pressed her lips together. His story sounded half-assed to say the least. Was there truth in anything he said?

He leaned toward her with a slight smile. His masculine scent, reminiscent of the alpine woods, tantalized her senses. What could be the harm in spending a little time with him? He had proven he had her best interests at heart, hadn't he? She didn't have any kind of fortune hidden away that he could be after.

She pushed her hair from her face. If he did have some ulterior motive, keeping him close topped the list of smart things to do.

He held out a hand. "Come on, Neva, let's get some dinner, a nice glass of wine, and take advantage of the music the band is playing. You like to dance, don't you?"

She searched his eyes. "Yes, I like dancing. All right, dinner sounds good, but I need to change out of this cold weather gear first. I'll meet you at the entrance to the dining room in, say, half an hour?"

He escorted her to the elevator and gave a two-fingered wave before the doors closed for her upward jaunt.

At the door to her room her hands trembled, making it difficult to get the key card to work. When the green light signaled, she hurried inside, tossing her bag onto the bed. She shrugged out of the now hot coat and sat down to tug off her boots. What to wear? She hadn't packed with the idea of sitting across a table from sexy Bane Heughar, or swaying in his arms to a piece of romantic music. A fluttery feeling tickled the inside of her stomach.

She took off the clothes she wore and tied her hair back. She managed a quick sponge bath, and then slipped on fresh underwear. With haste she rummaged through the clothes in her suitcase, tossing aside the ones that wouldn't do. With limited choices, she settled on a simple black skirt and silky button up blouse in a soft shade of slate. Hell, she sure hadn't brought dancing shoes. These strappy plum colored heels would have to do. Back in front of the bathroom mirror, she dashed on some eye shadow, applied a touch of lip gloss, and brushed her long hair until it lay across her shoulders at least halfway tamed.

Bane awaited her in front of the dining entrance. He had scrubbed up too and changed into a dark green shirt that made the flecks in his eyes sparkle like gold dust. He actually gave a low appreciative whistle as she walked toward him. "You look amazing, Neva." He offered his arm, and she took it with a smile.

Dinner conversation ran toward the ease of both their flights and the incomparable beauty of this spot in Norway. She didn't delve into his reasons for the trip, preferring not to prick any holes in his story bubble right now. Plus, there was a chance he acted in perfect sincerity when he said he wanted to get to know her better. She couldn't deny she liked being here with him. Her skin tingled each time he gave her one of his smoldering gazes, and every time he found reason to touch her.

As they sipped their after dinner wine, he leaned forward, and his finger grazed over her hand before coming to rest there. "Neva, why did you shoot off over here to Norway?"

"I-I had talked to my doctor before the sleepwalking incident, and to Granny Eastwick as well. They both encouraged me to look to my past for answers. Then..."

"Yes, go on."

She took a deep breath before answering. "I found information in a batch of old boxes belonging to my foster parents, the ones who took me in when I was seven and were killed soon after. Long story short, the intel led me to Norway. Tomorrow I'm going to Trollstigen, and hopefully I'll find what I need."

"May I accompany you?"

Her chin lifted. "I'd like that."

"What are you looking for so far from home?"

"Anything about my childhood or my real mother."

"Sometimes the past can be painful, Neva—and dangerous."

She furrowed her brow and curled her finger over his thumb. "I have to know. You understand that, don't you, Bane?"

His tender expression heated her cheeks. He nodded. "I understand. We all have things we have to do." A sudden grimace flashed across his features, and he clenched his fist.

"Your scar is hurting again. Let me see." She opened his fingers and cupped his hand. With a soft touch she traced the edges of the carving in the padded flesh. Then she placed her palm on top. "Let me try Reiki. It's a natural healing energy and may soothe the wound. Okay?"

An interested expression belied his shrug. "Sure, I'm game."

Closing her eyes, she touched in with her Reiki guide, Kashima, and channeled the energy while using the tip of her tongue to trace the first symbol onto the roof of her mouth, *Cho Ku Rei*. The pulsing blood of Bane's hand immediately leaped up in response to the symbol of power. *The warrior's life force is strong.* She continued with the next two symbols, *Sei Hei Ki* and *Hon Sha Ze Sho Nen*. She honored the formerly secret names of the symbols, repeating them over and over in her mind. She offered up tribute to the stations of power, as well as to Kashima, who directed her. After a few moments, the pulsing emanating from Bane's hand accelerated and heightened even further. She added the most sacred symbol, *Dai Ko Myo,* soul healer. Lightness in her heart chakra proclaimed it the right decision. She maintained the energy until Bane's leaping pulse quietened, signaling the end of the session.

Opening her eyes, she blinked under the scrutiny of his steady gaze. A slight smile tugged at the corners of his lips, and he reached out to trace her jaw with his fingertips. "That felt damn good." He flexed his fingers. "Thank you, Neva." Giving her hand a squeeze, he stood. "I promised you a dance. Shall we give it a whirl?"

* * * *

Bane's groin tightened as Neva came into his arms, flowing against him like water over a rock. He breathed in the perfume of her woman's body. It reminded him of the aroma of night blossoms scattered along the forest pathways where he used to ride his favorite horse in ancient Norway, before undergoing rebirth as a warrior in the Underworld. Neva's soft wildflower scent whispered rarity, all woman, and sexy as hell. The urgency of his Underworld mission receded, when all he wanted to do was stash Neva in his bed and make love to her all night long.

The sweet way she used her healing touch on him had almost brought him to his knees. No matter how hard he tried, he couldn't see her as a demoness. A lump formed in his throat as he recalled slipping Helle's potion into Neva's wine earlier when her attention had been riveted on the band. She had sipped the drink easily enough, and he couldn't discern any reaction whatsoever. Was Helle dead wrong about Neva or had the power of her demoness blood neutralized the magical elixir? Or did the concoction need time to settle, as Helle had suggested? He could only pray the potion activated to the good, and not to the bad, before the Solstice Moon.

With Neva in his arms, the music half hypnotized him. When her head came to rest against his shoulder, he put his lips against her ear. "I've never met anyone like you, Neva. You're a stunning woman. I see stars in your eyes, and there's a mystery about you that makes me want to…"

She tilted her face to his, her silvery eyes half-closed and glowing. "To what?"

Her full lips enticed him. "To kiss you." His mouth came down on hers, hungry and searching, and then flaming toward a savage passion so fast that his mind spun.

She broke away, her lips swollen, as if they were begging for more of his kisses. "Bane, w-we can't."

He stiffened, gazing dazed around the room. *Odin's balls.* How had he forgotten they were in a public area? This woman could make him forget his name if she put her mind to it. With a half laugh, he placed an arm around her shoulders. "Come on." Throwing some bills onto their table, he guided her out of the room and into the elevator. "What floor are you on?"

"Seven."

He couldn't resist taking her in his arms again. Her body melted against his like a dream, inflaming his senses. "Your lips make me crazy, Neva."

She murmured a whispered reply, while pressing soft kisses onto his cheek and throat. "Your talented mouth is to blame, Bane. It's scorching hot."

He pressed her hard against the wall, threading his fingers through the silk of her hair. "This mouth is just getting started. You'd be amazed at all it can do."

Her breath became ragged. "Is that a promise?" With half-closed eyes and biting her lower lip, she wrapped one leg around his waist.

His need to keep touching her intensified until he could only focus on the desirable woman in his arms.

Her passion seemed to match his. He was exploring the silky curves of her lower back when the elevator jolted to a stop and the doors swished open.

The four teenagers entering the elevator snickered, and one gave a little salute as Bane and Neva exited. Her rosy cheeks and swollen lips made Bane realize how tempting he found her and the overpowering effect she had on him. It was almost like being bewitched.

Pain jolted his hand just as a kernel of ice seemed to form in the pit of his stomach. No matter how lovely she was and how damn much he wanted her, more than he had ever wanted any woman in fact, the Underworld mission came first.

She gave him the key card and when she took his hand to pull him inside, he stopped her. "Neva, I think it's best we sleep on this…whatever this is."

She blinked several times. "Sleep on it? Y-you mean…you're going…"

He squeezed her shoulder. "We're getting a little carried away. We're jet lagged. Let's both get some *zzz*s, all right?"

He had experienced and dealt some punishing blows in his life, but walking away from Neva tonight proved the hardest thing he'd ever had to do.

* * * *

Neva snatched off her silky blouse, tossing it on the bed. After sipping the wine she had poured, she stared at herself in the mirror. What had possessed her to wear this fancy laced cobalt-blue bra? Bane would never see her in it. He had made it clear he wouldn't touch her if the end of the world loomed near. With a finger she traced the curve of the top of her breast, watching herself in the mirror. Not too bad. She might have wished for that champagne shape lauded over in books, and hers weren't quite that round looking, but they would do in a pinch.

A slight moan escaped her as she pictured Bane's finger touching her breast instead of her own. With a violent tug, she unzipped her skirt and stomped it off, giving it a little kick at the end. Why had he acted so contrary anyway? She hadn't asked him to marry her, for Goddess sake. Everyone went for a roll in the hay these days without a lot of fuss. Of course she hadn't had much experience, but she did hope to rectify that. She looked at the mirror again, trying to be objective. Far from gorgeous, neither was she hideous. Maybe he just didn't like women.

Now that idea had never occurred to her—until now. Surely Bane didn't prefer men. The way he had kissed her came close to nuclear with its heat and intensity. His mouth on hers made her feel ravished. She couldn't imagine him raining kisses down on another man, putting his hands on him, pulling down his shorts.

Heat flooded her belly at the image. Apparently she could imagine it. She swallowed at her shortness of breath. Grabbing the wine glass, she took a big swallow of the succulent red liquid. Heat suffused her body. Tilting her head back, she swayed a little from side to side, soft sensuous music playing in her head. Putting her hands at the sides of her thong, she slid the garment down a little, running her thumbs over the hardness of her hipbones. Molten heat filled her womanly core, and she fluttered a hand across her triangular patch. Oh my goddess, it was scorching in here. She reached behind and unclasped her bra.

The door swung open.

Neva froze.

Bane stood at the entrance, his eyes grazing her breasts and lowering, coming to rest on her disheveled state of undress.

"How did you open that door? I had the safety latch on." She cringed at the breathy sound of her voice.

"Apparently it didn't catch. Sorry..." His eyes swept over her, searing her skin with flashes of heat. "Forgive my barging in. I did knock." He held up her bag. "I forgot I carried this for you. I thought you might need it."

When his gaze lifted to meld with hers, the heat she had longed to see in him singed her to the bone. He looked like he could devour her right now.

She gasped as he moved in front of her, not touching her with his body. "You might as well not have a stitch on as these damn blue scraps." His voice rasped with deep unadulterated lust.

The same lust that had overcome her while thinking of him, and caused her to dance alone, lower her panties, and unclasp her bra.

Still not touching her with his body, Bane cupped her face in his hands, pressing his mouth onto hers. The kiss defied convention and gentility. His tongue assaulted hers, pooling lava into her center. She parried back, savoring the attack, reveling in the mating of their mouths.

She drowned in the intensity of his kiss. Every nerve came alive in her body, and electrical stinging sensations prickled up and down her skin. Then she needed more. His mouth wasn't enough, not nearly enough, and she leaned into him with her ripe, aroused body. Her already erect nipples stiffened to nubs, as the hardness of his chest grazed them through the sheer lace of her bra.

His hands slid to her back, where the bra opening dangled. He broke away from her mouth to whisper sweet words, his voice harsh and strange with all the blood pulsating in her ears. "I tried to stay away from you tonight."

She quivered as his lips brushed against her throat.

"Tell me you want me as much as I want you."

"Yes, oh yes, I-I want you, Bane."

His body shook with a concentrated power she hadn't experienced in a man. It made her want to melt against him and give him everything he needed.

Then, as if it took great willpower, he squeezed his eyes shut, clasped her arms, and thrust her away. "You've had too much wine. You don't know what you're doing, and I won't take advantage of you, though Odin knows it's the only thing on the green earth I want to do right now. I'll see you in the morning for the Trollstigen trip." He traced a finger around her jawline. "Goodnight, Neva."

Hell no. Neva's chest heaved as he closed the door behind him, her body still vibrating with the torchy desire he had ignited in her. Although she couldn't think straight, his reference to Odin rang in her ears. What did it mean? Why would Bane use the name of an ancient Norse god in such a way? Doubt and curiosity rooted her to the spot. Where did Bane come from—really? Who the hell was he, and what did he want with her? If Odin were his patron god, it seemed fitting to suspect he had fae blood running in his veins. Truth be told, she had wondered about it more than once. And now, Bane had followed her to

Norway. And then set her aside. Left her bereft and alone. Why?

Chapter Eight

Neva breathed in the clean smell of snow. Snow?

Oh my goddess, I've been sleepwalking again.

She looked around, bewildered. Howling roared behind her, and dread swamped over her like quicksand. Where in the hell was she? She hurried away from the howling sound, while glancing around to get her bearings. Snow covered the ground as far as she could see. She had apparently walked for quite a distance and reached a higher elevation. She remembered climbing into bed in the little room she had rented in Valldal. She and Bane had taken the car and then the ferry toward the Troll's Path the morning after he had rejected her. Other than make a big scene and bare her heart, she had no choice but to pretend his rebuff also meant nothing to her.

Yet it did. He had held her close, seemed to want her with the same fierce abandon as she wanted him. Then he pushed her away. Her heart hurt, and she didn't have the slightest idea what to do about it.

Added to that were her suspicions about his possible supernatural heritage. Despite how he had come to her rescue before, she couldn't trust him. He had some ulterior motive where she was concerned. If she could just figure out the truth.

As for him, he carried on as if nothing major had happened between them.

Now here she was sleepwalking again. Her malady had stuck her out in the middle of nowhere. The howling sound came closer. She trudged faster. Whatever stalked her was not only noisy, but huge. Its breath whiffed at the back of her head and she caught a bad scent, like rotten eggs. Then she ran.

Whoomp. The creature raced behind her. Even in the snow its gait created thumping sounds. Whether natural or supernatural, she had no doubt it wanted to harm her, possibly kill her. Snorts of puffy air hit her back, forming hovering clouds a few feet above the ground. Despite her speed, the icy air still permeated her body and her being. She could no longer feel her hands inside the gloves.

She fixated on a morbid desire to see what the creature looked like. Should she stop, turn around, and face it? Inexorable panic in the pit of her stomach swamped her, its acid claws warming her for a split second before the cold took over again. If she stopped, whatever chased her would catch up in seconds. Damned if she'd let despair and weariness bring about her premature demise. Not a chance. She'd keep running until her breath and bones gave out. No galloping thumps sounded behind her now. Had she out distanced the creature?

She kept moving. Up ahead a swirl of lights caught her attention. *The northern lights? So beautiful.* Despite her flight and her uncertainty as to whether or not the creature still pursued, her heart swelled to meet the brilliant greens and reds undulating like gigantic orchestra lights. In fact, music seemed to accompany them. The melody reminded her of Mussorgsky, *Night on Bald Mountain* perhaps. If she could just get to the lights, she'd be safe. No loathsome creature could exist in the presence of such beauty.

With her gaze uplifted, transfixed on the ethereal lights, her foot landed on a rock, turned, and down she tumbled. Down and farther down. Unable to regain her footing, she rolled down a steep decline. She hadn't noticed the treacherous drop off. Snow encircled her body, and she fought to tuck in her arms and legs so as not to break a bone. Her mind fogged up with the sensation of being tumbled in a dryer. How steep was this damn hill anyway? She slid onward, rushing, rushing, down and down. *Clomp.* The ground bumped beneath her, and after another few seconds, her body thudded to a stop.

Neva panted, desperate to catch her breath. After a few moments, she drew in a ragged siphon of air. She blinked at the whiteness all around her. Apparently a snowbank encased her. Hysterical laughter threatened to take over. She imagined the headline now. "Neva Jaxony, Artist, Meets Demise Inside Giant Snowball."

Hell no. She'd claw her way out even if she were under a dozen feet of snow. Her shortness of breath increased, along with her hysteria. She placed a palm over her heart.

Calm down.

She needed to relax.

She closed her eyes and focused on the Goddess of the northern lights, the great Freya. "Great Mother Goddess, please help me. Calm me and take me unto your heart, that I may be freed from this snowy prison."

A feeling of peace flowed over her, followed by the certainty that she could get out of this situation. A voice inside her head reminded her to use the power of her hands. *As you have done before, Neva.* Hadn't her hands generated heat like an ambient candle glow, not a burning heat but a soothing, healing warmth? She naturally gravitated toward using their heat for minor bruises and cuts and had been thrilled to receive Reiki attunement and training from Granny Eastwick. She had used the energy channeled through her hands to stop a bleeding episode when Granny Eastwick cut a finger. Recently she had eased the inflamed scar on Bane's palm.

So, maybe she could use her hands now.

"Divine Mother Goddess, and Kashima, my Reiki guide, I call on your healing energy as directed from you into my crown chakra, through my heart chakra, and on into my hands. Help them to generate genuine heat to deflect and melt this encasement of snow."

When the heat surged into her palms and the vibrations of energy began, she flexed her fingers and touched the snow. The snow seemed to give way a little, and she pushed up at it. Before long, her hands had progressed upward to the level of her forehead. She continued the pressure until able to move her legs. Rising on her knees she resumed pushing at the snow. *It's a part of the divine mother, the snow is, and within my realm to command.* A blissful feeling surged within. The Goddess had granted her the power to extricate herself from this icy prison.

Soon she could stand up. With both hands she gave a sweeping swirl parallel to her body, and surged free. Gulping in huge breaths, the gallons it seemed she needed, she panted and gazed at her surroundings. White everywhere. She stood at the bottom of a mountain. Well, more like a foothill but what a marvel she had survived the roll down its steep decline. "Thank you, divine Mother Goddess."

Now what? She had no idea of her location. Her disjointed thoughts meandered. This scene would be easy to paint—just a blank canvas and a few drops of silver glitter needed. She chortled at her giddy joke, and then tried to be serious. Maybe the fall had shaken her off kilter. Or even off her trolley. She laughed again.

Oh my goddess, am I getting frostbite? Snow sickness? True, she couldn't feel her hands, even though they had been hot just a few moments before. It dawned on her that she had to get to a place of warmth. Leave the exposure of the open mountain. The wind blew in forceful gusts. She fell to her knees, and it took all her strength to stand up again. She could no longer see the northern lights. The snow blinded her. The wind took away her breath. Images tumbled across one another in her mind.

If she made it through this, she'd invest in a running program to keep in shape. She'd been doing a lot of painting and drawing lately and hadn't had enough exercise. Not that being fleet footed would really help here. A hysterical giggle escaped her lips. Either these inane thoughts were an effort to keep her brain occupied or she had an inch of control left before going bonkers. She'd vote for the former.

Hunched over, she made her way toward a dark shape in the distance. It looked parallel to where she now walked. It could be a mirage but she hoped not. She prayed it was a ledge or opening where she could warm up her body before it went into full-blown temperature shock.

Thank you, Goddess. After what seemed like a century she made out the dark blotch as a gaping aperture in the mountain. Her heart thudded. It looked like a cave. Her panicky intuition had led her here. Could this be the onyx cavern mentioned in Jewel's diary?

It was a cave, or at least an opening. She had to lean down and step over a foot of slush to get inside. With the heavy snow plummeting down, she worried how long it would take for the entrance to be fully barricaded. She'd have to keep an eye on it and not let that happen. To be trapped inside a cave would be just as bad as to be trapped outside in the elements. First things first. How far did this cave go into the side of the mountain, and did it go up, down, or straight ahead?

She made her way into the interior of the cave, wishing she had a flashlight. Why hadn't her sleepwalking escapade included a penlight and proper supplies? No food. No water. No light. An eerie feeling swept over her. This scenario sucked big time.

She continued slogging into the cave. It had tapered until only two people would fit abreast in here. Its shape conformed to that of a finger. The path turned and meandered, and she followed it for several minutes before the opening expanded to a larger space.

Her stomach lurched at the strange and magnificent panorama surrounding her, truly an alien world. "Oh, my goddess, am I dreaming?" Her words and exhalations formed frosty clouds that floated around her body.

Black crystals studded the dome shaped space. Some were opaque and some transparent. They hung down from the ceiling of the cave and erupted from the ground—brilliant stalactites and stalagmites of all shapes and sizes. She didn't know such dark crystals existed. The ones she had seen in pictures were either clear or frosty. Her hand fluttered to her heart.

Torches hung like sentries all along the walls. Where the torchlight shone on the crystals, the black hues banded off into sparkles of red, blue, green, and even purple.

It was as if the northern lights had slipped inside this cave, mated with the ice, and formed the inimitable dark crystals of the onyx cavern.

The cold seeped from her body. Slowly, she thawed out in this warmer, cocooned space inside the mountain. She found a hunk of blunted rock, a stalagmite that had not formed its point but rather lumbered along the ground in a perfect semblance of a comfortable little settee. She sat down, rubbing her hands together. A thousand pins pricked at her skin as the feeling began to return. She had read the extremities of hands and feet were the most prone to frostbite. She rubbed her face to stimulate the blood. Maybe she ought to remove her boots and socks to check on her feet.

She didn't know what she'd find when she did that though or how she'd react if frostbite had already claimed a toe, so she settled on gently stomping her feet on the ground, one at a time, to try and bring back circulation. At the same time she continued to massage her hands.

She sank down to rest for a bit, taking care not to doze off. Afterward she'd return to the entrance and make sure it remained clear of snow. A few minutes of peace followed while she sat and admired the colorful crystal display. While perusing the stones, her eyes widened and then she squinted, peering into what could only be a mirage.

Oh my goddess.

Surging to her feet she tottered and climbed over stalagmites to reach the strange sight. It had to be an illusion. She could only see a part of it. If she could just get around this rock. She did, and the spectacle that met her eyes made her heart race.

Inside a tall stalagmite stood a woman.

The woman had ice blonde hair, lips that held a distinct blue tinge, and lighter toned bluish skin. Neva expected a frozen body to look wizened and corpselike, but this one didn't. Her lips were still plump. She looked peaceful and regal, as a queen might. With her eyes closed, she appeared to be dead, frozen, or perhaps sleeping.

What a crazy thought. Certainly it couldn't be a woman sleeping. Maybe a traveler had been caught in a sudden ice storm and frozen solid. Neva frowned, dismissing the idea. The woman's clothing suggested bygone days. A long flowing gown of royal blue, gathered above the waist and garnished with jewels, gave her the appearance of a forgotten queen from a long ago age.

Did an ice crystal or a translucent onyx formation like the others in the cave encase the woman? Stunned, Neva continued to stare at the strange sight before her. Thoughts collided in her mind. From out of the dark came a certainty as she studied the ethereal form before her. She had to be some type of fae creature, trapped and hidden away. Neva reached out and touched the side of the crystal.

As her fingers came in contact with the onyx formation encasing the mysterious woman, an electric shock zapped through her hand. She jerked away from the dark stone. What the hell? The crystal acted like a conduit or conductor. Did the energy originate from her recently used Reiki or had magic taken over?

Swallowing, she reached out again, this time with one finger only. *Zap!* She jerked away, flinching at the energy spasm. She peered at her finger. The power surge had left a red mark. She frowned in puzzlement. What on earth was going on here?

To her astonishment, the crystal where she had touched it with her hands and then with the tip of her finger now slurped down and warped in those very spots. It did not melt as ice would melt. The electricity had jolted her to the extent that she couldn't tell if the crystal radiated an icy cold. *Okay, this is screwy.* A little voice told her to get the hell away from the frozen woman. Another voice, her curiosity she supposed, refused to let her off the hook. *Holy hell.* Which message was angelic, and which was not?

Cocking her arm and gritting her teeth, she touched the tip of her elbow to the crystal. No zap this time, just a low tremor in the crystal. A vibration.

Oh, the hell with it.

Clamping her lips together, she put her palms close to the crystal without touching it. The crystal warped. There was no zap, but the energy she was accustomed to feeling when she used Reiki was that which now flowed through her hands. She gasped at the result. The warping phenomenon increased.

She jerked her hands away again. Whatever the woman was, whatever or whomever had confined her here—did she really want to take a chance on the prisoner becoming free? What if she had been captured and left here for a good cause? What if she wasn't dead but was in some kind of suspended animation or altered state? It sounded like a sci-fi movie.

She touched the crystal again.

With a sudden flash the woman's eyes opened wide.

Neva jumped back in shock.

The woman's gaze shifted and gelled on Neva's, and her mouth moved. "Help me."

No voice sounded, but Neva read the lips with ease. Was she dreaming or experiencing reality? She had no sense of a dream or illusion, but could she actually tell anymore? The woman seemed alive and desperate for assistance. How could Neva do otherwise but place her hands in position again, hovering over the crystal?

Within minutes the crystal had melted, one side of it oozing to the ground as if it were candle wax. It formed its own kind of peculiar stalagmite. Neva stepped away.

The woman jerked forward, looking like the tin man receiving oil after a century or so. Her chest heaved, and the sound of a great ragged breath cut into the room, reverberating off the crystals in the cavern. It sounded to Neva's ears more like a great cave bear aroused from hibernation than a person waking from sleep.

She wrung her hands together. What had she done?

The former captive made an utterance that could have been an effort at speech. It came out more like a rusty grunt. With a wave of her arms, she pushed aside the half molten crystal in front of her and moved forward, stepping over the residue that had built up like a low rising stalagmite on the floor. She released a shuddering breath and took another.

Her skin began to take on more of a flesh tone, although her lips remained bluish.

Neva clapped a hand over her mouth, as a serpentine blue line appeared and curved across one side of the woman's face from forehead to chin. There it wound its way lower to disappear beneath the fabric of her gown. It had the appearance of a plump vein very near the surface of the skin. Her loveliness remained but now exuded a more alien aspect with the blue vein meandering on her creamy flesh.

"Ahh, how delicious it is to breathe again, to move my limbs."

The woman spoke in a strange language, but Neva had no trouble understanding her. Granny Eastwick had told her about the innate fae ability to comprehend foreign languages. Did she now have firsthand knowledge of the magical gift?

The regal mysterious creature nodded at Neva and offered a smile. "Thank you."

Neva swallowed. "Who are you?"

"My name is Skada."

"Skada. That's unusual."

"You haven't heard of me?"

"Not that I recall. Should I have?"

The woman pursed her lips and nodded.

At a loss, Neva questioned. "Why's that? Why should I have heard of you?"

Skada's eyes flared with heat. "I was once a renowned Goddess—feared by some, revered by many. Times have changed."

"Why were you—were you...?" Her voice faltered.

"Imprisoned in the onyx cavern, my own home?" Skada's tone tightened to anger. "My enemies wanted to be rid of me. Now they'll realize I'm not so easily disposed of."

"Oh." Neva couldn't think of a response to that. She had feared a justifiable confinement. Maybe Skada didn't deserve to be imprisoned, but Neva worried that she had let loose a dark unnatural force onto the world.

"Don't look so stricken. You did the right thing."

Neva found her voice. "What did you do to cause your enemies to put you here?"

"I lived and thrived. They could not tolerate my success."

"You're not...evil?"

The woman laughed outright. "I'd hardly admit it, would I?"

Neva grimaced.

"Forgive a small amount of sarcastic humor. No, of course I don't consider myself evil. Any more than you do. Does anyone, actually?"

Neva's chin jerked up. It seemed as if the woman had read her mind, cut straight through the gloom and worry she had experienced after the recent unsettling incidents.

"Come here, child."

Swallowing, Neva took a step closer.

Skada reached out and touched her cheek with a long nailed finger. "Who are you?"

Reluctance weighed her down. Her voice croaked out in a whisper. "Neva Jaxony."

The woman hissed and jerked back as if shocked. "Neva Jaxony. Indeed." Her ice grey eyes took on the brilliance of stars. They burned into Neva.

"I called for you, Neva Jaxony."

"What do you mean, called for me?"

Skada reached for Neva's trembling hand, held it for a moment, and then released it. Her expression softened a bit. "I called for you through my blood, frozen with time and by supernatural means. We are of the same origin. Fae blood older than the earth herself. I am your mother."

Chapter Nine

Neva's hand flew to her mouth. "No! That's impossible. You can't be my mother."

Skada's face tightened. "Did Jewel Orsen not tell you about the mother who left you with her for safe keeping?"

"I never knew Jewel. I think she and her husband died when I was a baby."

"A baby. So Jewel Orsen did not live to raise you. What happened to you after she died?"

"I honestly don't know. I only recently found out about Jewel. A couple named Remy took me in about age seven. Before that...I-I have no memory."

"Another crime for which my enemies must pay. My daughter grew up orphaned with me imprisoned here in this forsaken Underworld cell."

Neva didn't know what to say. She couldn't seem to take it all in. Tears threatened to spill from her soul. She held her breath, determined to hold them back.

Skada cupped her chin. "Are you not pleased to discover your mother is alive?"

"Yes, of course, but I don't want to believe it and then find out it's not true."

"Oh, but it is true." She wrapped her arms around Neva, hugging her.

The woman's body temperature exuded cold, like a slab of melting ice. Neva shivered.

Stepping back, Skada's brow furrowed. "I see it will take a little doing for us to get acquainted. That's quite all right. For you I have time to spare."

"Your body is so cold. We need to get you warmed up. Here, take my coat."

Skada smiled, slipping her arms through the sleeves. "Mmm. This is nice." She wrapped the coat tight around her, hugging it to her slender frame. "Do you believe I'm your mother now?"

"You're too powerful to be my mother."

Skada laughed, the tinkling sound cascading off the crystals. "You don't think you're powerful, my daughter?"

Neva's eyes widened. "Not in a good way. I'm...different."

Skada swept Neva's hair back off the shoulder. "Who told you that?"

"My foster parents, all of them, one after another, always said I looked and acted a fright. Also, I have a mind of my own."

Skada chortled again. This time it sounded less mirthful and more perfunctory. "Without meaning to, those idiots paid you a compliment. To be different is a miraculous advantage. If you see me as powerful, you must learn to think so of yourself as well, for in many ways you take after me. You have qualities of your father in you as well. Exquisite does not begin to describe him. Combined, our powers achieved heights beyond the imagination. Open your mind, Neva. Your self-image is distorted by the lies of banal people."

Neva gasped. She hadn't even considered her father.

Skada nodded. "Your father was called Jaz. I gave you a semblance of his name."

"This is a lot to take in."

"I'm aware." Skada shivered and rubbed her arms through the coat.

"We need to find a way to get you warm."

"I should be able to generate palpable heat once I've rested and rejuvenated. Let's recline against these rocks for a few moments. Talk to me, child. What have you been doing with your life? Are you adept in the magical arts?"

Neva frowned. "I haven't known of my fae heritage for long but am learning what it means to be a Wytchfae. As far as I know, I'm not adept at summoning or spells. I use a pendulum and Reiki, but Reiki is a natural act, only supernatural if you think the world itself is magical."

"That's partially true. The world is magical and based on mysterious mathematics that most people call daily living. But there's also a deeper sorcery to be found. Your fae power will soon surge forth to escape its confines. You hail from an ancient, powerful bloodline. Surely you have had experiences that made you question your place in the everyday world. Am I right?"

Neva's breath came short, thinking of all that had happened to her recently. "I've had strange dreams—horrible nightmares really—and weird incidents."

"Ahh, lucid dreams. Perhaps you are a dream walker. We must pursue the matter and find out. Come with me now. Let's depart this place and seek a safe haven to pursue the matter of your heritage."

"Hopefully the snowfall isn't blocking the exit."

Skada extended a palm. A tendril of dark blue light flared out from it, a mere trickle that expanded into an elongated form and skittered down the dim corridor toward the direction Neva had entered. "Is that corridor how you emerged into the cavern?"

"Yes, I tumbled down a hill into a snowbank, managed to get free, and then stumbled onto the entrance of this cave."

"It's no accident you found me in this Underworld cell in old Norway, Neva. It's fate that you came here and freed me from my imprisonment."

Perhaps Skada spoke the truth. This whole experience had the quality of a dream. Everything seemed surreal. Could Skada really be her mother? Could she have been fated to take a trip to Norway and find her? Free her from her prison? She frowned. "Is this really the Underworld or were you speaking metaphorically?"

"Oh, yes. It is a section of the Underworld and therefore part of the cobweb of real estate that my dear sister governs. As an additional measure, she sent me back in time as well."

Neva's mouth fell open. "We're in another time? And your sister did this to you?"

"Yes, my sister Helle. You've heard of her?"

"Only in myths and stories."

"You hadn't heard of me."

"Actually now that you mention it again, I do remember a name similar to yours in some of the old tales."

Skada looked pleased. "Good. I'm glad Helle and Eshigel, the Guardian of the Between, couldn't obliterate my legacy. What are the stories?"

Neva frowned to remember. "I don't recall much. A giantess with a name similar to yours lived in the frozen north."

Skada waved a jeweled hand and shook her head. "As you can see, I am tall but not unduly so. Oh well, one cannot control the growth of legends or folk stories over the mists of time. At least my name lived on. You didn't hear of atrocities attributed to me or learn the details of my imprisonment?"

"No, nothing of that sort."

"Very well. I will enlighten you once we are in a place of safety."

"Do you fear Helle will come after you again?"

"I am certain she will send the hounds of the netherworld for me. Nor are you safe."

"Why? What does she have against you? Why did she imprison you in the first place?"

"As I said there's a lot to tell. My strength returns. Let us leave this pit of danger before all else."

"I wish I had my camera with me to take pictures of this onyx cave before I leave it. It's the most fascinating place I've ever seen. I'd like to get it on canvas."

"You're an artist?"

"Yes, I paint with oils and acrylics. I mostly paint my dreams."

Skada nodded approvingly. "I am proud of that quality in you, my daughter."

Neva swallowed. "Thank you…Mother."

A bright smile flitted across Skada's face. An immediate glare off into the distance shadowed it. "Together we shall exact vengeance on those who imprisoned me, and harmed you in the process."

Neva's heartbeat increased. The single word hissed from her lips like steam. "Vengeance?"

Skada nodded. "It's the only way we can assure our safety. As well, my dear daughter, it is much like the sweetest wine. If you haven't tasted it yet, you will." With a violent thrust, she flung out her arms. "Step aside that I may bore an exit."

In the next moment a great rumbling knocked Neva to the ground.

Some of the crystals jerked free of the walls and moved, their points becoming legs and hands, huge gaping maws opening where a face would be. They sped toward Skada.

Neva screamed and scrambled out of the way. She cringed at the sight of their horrifying apertures.

Skada shrieked, the sound reverberating throughout the cavern. "No! You are my soldiers-- *mine*. You cannot turn against me."

* * * *

A searing sensation in his palm woke Bane. Helle's damn rune. He may as well have had a hot poker stuck in his flesh. He stumbled from the narrow bed, stifling a groan. Grabbing a can of antiseptic spray from his bag, he slathered his hand and obtained a towel from the bathroom to wind around it. His heart softened at the memory of Neva's gentle healing touch. The last thing he wanted to do was awaken her, asking for more. She needed her rest to face what lay ahead.

Heaviness settled in his chest at the task Helle required of him. The killing scythe seemed to bore a hole in his inner pocket. How could he kill Neva? The urge to check on her overwhelmed him. He'd just go now and make sure she slept undisturbed.

Making his way to her room, he flung out his hand and used magic to unlock the door. Slipping inside, he peered in, expecting to see her cuddled beneath a pile of blankets. Instead, the covers were half on the floor. His heart pounded. The bed stood empty, as did the room. A quick search told him that her coat and wraps were missing. She had gone outside. She'd never go out alone in the middle of the night in her right mind. She had to be sleepwalking again—or worse. Damn it all to hell!

In frantic haste he ran back to his room and dressed, making sure to fill his pockets with his own weapons and the ones Helle had provided. He tied the magic kit to his belt and pulled his winter clothing over the top. Through the window the snowfall looked an intimidating sight. How would he track her? Opening his coat again and pulling up his sweater, he removed a small knife from the magic kit. He pulled the blade from the sheath by its intricate handle, carved with Odin's rune.

A directional athame. With such a magical knife he would be able to follow Neva's general path. He flicked a lighter and heated the blade, then set it down flat on the floor. With Helle's painful rune still throbbing, he held his hand a foot above the blade. "Great Odin, guide me to her."

The knife began to spin in slow motion, and then faster, faster, until its movement blurred into a shining translucence.

With a flash of light, the knife stopped. It pointed north, further toward Trollstigen. Bane resheathed the athame and secured it back in the kit. He slung his emergency bag over his arm, glad for the water and rations. He doubted Neva had any with her. His heart heavy with worry and a sense of foreboding, he set out after her.

Whether to kill or save her, he didn't know.

Although the falling snow left none of Neva's footprints for him to follow, confidence in the accuracy of the magical athame led him up the mountain. The logic of it made sense. Discovering the truth of her past had been foremost in Neva's mind. She wanted nothing more than to find the onyx cavern, if such a place existed.

He suspected it did exist as the location where Helle had imprisoned Skada. By sending her back in time, Helle would have made sure Skada served aeons instead of mere years.

If the cave stood intact and accessible, he had an inkling Neva would be drawn there. By Odin, he prayed for her safety.

After walking for an hour, he stopped long enough to swallow down some water and take a belt of brandy to ward off the frigid cold. As he gained altitude, the temperature plummeted.

Then he yanked the cap down over his ears and resumed his journey. He followed the pathway of trolls in fair fashion under the midnight sun. Did she stick to the road, though, or did the onyx cavern jut off where the terrain lumbered into the side of the mountain?

Putting his left hand over his chest, he spoke to his patron god. "Odin, great father, guide me to her." The pulsing of Odin's rune drummed on his flesh as it attuned to the beat of his own heart. At the next footpath leading off the main route, Bane veered away from the central road and headed toward where Odin led him.

The snow reached waist high, and he slogged through it, gasping for breath. Pushing against it sapped his strength. Still, he kept going, his mind open for Odin to guide him toward whatever lay ahead.

From the shadows of the cliffs came a hissing growl, rushing over his head, as if the rocks themselves emitted the noise. Maybe the sound came from the north wind whipping up. No such luck. In seconds the sound rubbed against the hairs on the back of his neck. Then it came at him from three sides, moving closer and faster. *Odin's balls.* He was in for a fight. Sliding his sword from its scabbard, he gripped a short blade in the other hand and turned to face the multiple threats.

The first ice troll reached him from the left. The creature's spiky talons sprang straight out several feet from its oversized mitt. Bluish in color, the creature looked like a mad mishmash between a lumbering lowland ogre and a gigantic highland snow beast. It moved faster and with more angular dexterity than either. Encumbered by his heavy clothing, Bane crouched in order to match his stability to the troll's spins and parries.

When it lifted its massive arm as if to rake its talons across his chest, he swerved to the side and cut upward at the creature from below. The arm fell off just above the elbow.

The creature grabbed its wound. The ground shook as it fell down with roars of agony.

The foul aroma of ichorous demon blood assailed his nostrils. He'd wager these were not natural ice trolls. His warrior's sense told him someone had set them here as sentry to guard the onyx cavern. If so, Neva had to be somewhere close by.

A second troll made a flying leap at him from a ledge above. He crouched down, holding the sword up like a spear. He let go of the weapon as it impaled his opponent. He flung himself to the side to avoid being crushed. Rolling, he latched onto a fir stump to keep from going over the precipice. How had he edged so close to the cliff?

Before he had time to catch his breath, regain his footing, or retrieve the sword, the third troll lurched at him. The creature ran fast, displaying an off kilter but effective gait.

With his short blade, Bane held onto the fir stump and jabbed at the troll low to the ground. His arm jolted as he clutched the blade. The creature shrieked and tumbled over the edge.

His chest heaving, Bane got to his feet and extracted his sword from the second troll. Both it and the first one lay still.

Soon the snowfall would cover them. He leaned against a tree and swigged water. By the time he capped the canteen, he was ready to resume his search. Before he took more than a few steps, the ground shook—not just the land below him, but the side of the mountain. Magic had burst wide open.

A bellowing shriek rang through the night. Spotting an opening in the hillside, Bane ran headlong into the bowels of the earth, toward the unholy sound.

Rocks tumbled around him. Thanks be to Odin this part of the path appeared as one serpentine corridor instead of an underground maze as in Helle's domain.

The path ended in a keyhole shaped dome, and it seemed clear that all hell had broken loose. The erratic shrieking came from a blue veined woman in the midst of a sea of dark and moving crystals. With arms akimbo and gliding in sinister fashion, they inexorably trapped her into the middle of their circle.

On second glance Bane discerned no ordinary woman but some kind of supernatural creature. Obsidian   wings   protruded   from   her   back.

Understanding hit him. The sorceress Skada stood before him. How had she awakened?

A sob brought his attention to a crumpled figure alongside the wall. *Neva!* He rushed to help her rise. He winced, touching blood that trickled down her cheek. "Something gashed your forehead."

She collapsed against the cavern wall and swept the outside of her hand over the wound. She stared at the blood on her hand. "Those crystal things came to life and knocked me onto a broken piece of rock. W-what are they?"

"Guards for this place, over that creature, apparently. Is that Skada?"

Neva straightened. "She's my mother—they've got her."

Gripping her shoulders, he stopped her from rushing into the melee.

"She didn't have wings before. Oh my goddess, I have to help her!"

"We can't prevent the guards from carrying out their divine duty. They are entrusted with dispensing justice for the atrocities Skada committed and the pain she inflicted with her sorcery. Don't you see what's happening? They are imprisoning her again."

As the crystal men reached out for Skada, a gelatinous film closed around her and then solidified. The face of the sorceress froze into a contortion of rage, her eyes fierce with hatred, her teeth bared in the midst of a scream of fury.

The sentinels stopped, apparently satisfied with their achievement, and in unison turned toward Bane and Neva.

The creatures shuffled forward. At the same time, the ground lurched with a vehement sideways motion. Both Bane and Neva were knocked off their feet.

He ignored the searing pain of Helle's rune in the palm of his hand. "Come on!" He jerked Neva upright. "We have to get out of here—now!"

Chapter Ten

Pulling Neva behind him, Bane raced down the serpentine corridor. He gained distance from the supernatural sentinels that wanted to imprison them. Desperate to get Neva to safety, his instincts took over. With pebbles and huge rocks falling like missiles, he whisked her away from the furious shaking of the earth, and toward the opening where he had first entered the onyx cavern.

With a leap, the two of them tumbled out into the snowbank. At least they were clear of the dangerous turmoil inside the cave. Sounds of destruction continued to echo, but the ground had stilled. Although he saw no evidence one way or another, he hoped they were back in the present day.

He helped Neva to her feet.

She shoved at his chest. "That was my mother in there."

"A black hearted sorceress, Neva. One too dangerous to be allowed her freedom." He gasped as

Neva swept hair out of her face. A blue vein like her mother's slashed up her cheek from her chin to her brow line.

The transformation had started. He had to get her out of here.

A pain shot through his hand as if a spear had pierced it. He fell to one knee.

She leaned over him. "What's the matter with you?"

Swallowing hard against the agony, he clenched his fingers and thrust his hand into his pocket. "It's not important. Let's get you out of this weather." He propelled her toward the path away from Trollstigen.

A radiant gleam up ahead caught his attention. No beam of light appeared. The glow didn't stem from the midnight sun, but rather seemed to emanate from the snow on the ground. His stomach lurched with dread.

From the icy ground rose up a dozen or more fire demons. Thin, but more than eight feet tall, their flames flickered red and yellow, and their eyes glowed. The hissing noise they made as they burned sounded like a pit full of vipers.

His voice rasped. "Damnation! Helle sent her army for us."

Neva clutched at his arm. "The Underworld Goddess?"

The creatures' long fingers extended and sizzled with electric blue streaks, and the fire talons reached for Bane and Neva.

He thrust Neva behind him.

Her arms tugged at him. "Bane, what the hell?"

The strong aroma of jasmine almost suffocated him, and a chilling voice reverberated through the air. "You disappoint me, warrior. My salamander flame brigade, bring these two traitors to me at once."

The fire demons merged the blue flames of all their talons to create a circle around Bane and Neva. The last one to join flicked his blazing arm and tossed a circle of gold fire into the air. Like bits of a hologram, the circle fanned out into a slinky shape that joined end to end and then grew larger and larger. With a booming sound, the vortex encompassed all of them. It swept them up into its swirling centrifugal force.

Bane grabbed Neva. His insides pitched to his throat as he tumbled in the midst of the vortex. The tumultuous swirling seemed as though it never would end, and the raucous explosive noise pressed down on his eardrums.

Then they landed with a great thud on a blanket of sharp rocks. A flat slate area lay ahead, almost like a platform. They appeared to be in a grotto of some sort. He grimaced. Probably one of Helle's peripheral locales where she received undesirables.

The salamander army of fire demons receded behind them.

Bane glanced back to see them standing more or less at attention, pulsating with their intense energy. He tugged Neva up with him and tucked her beneath his arm.

Even with her hair in spiky disarray, her clothes disheveled, dried blood matted on her lip, and the wicked blue vein marring her face, she was still the loveliest, most fascinating woman in all the thirteen worlds.

Terror shone from her eyes as she looked up at him. "Bane, why did they bring us here?"

He tried to smile at her. "I have a feeling Helle wants us dead."

She blinked at him and snuggled a shade closer.

A swishing sound drew his attention to the slate platform. It opened and Helle rose up from the ground, looking magnificent and inexorable. Despite the obvious wrath that seethed from her pores, her face remained as smooth and set as a death mask.

Her countenance sent icy chills up his spine. For the first time Helle's resemblance to her demonic sister Skada appeared all too evident. Even her body looked bristly, as if it were about to fly apart into poisoned tipped shards.

* * * *

Aware of Bane's tension beside her, Neva stared at the terrifying Goddess looming before them. The sweet scent of jasmine swept over her and brought on a sense of vertigo. She planted her feet to keep from tumbling over. For some reason Helle wanted them dead. She couldn't fathom why, but her mother had to be involved. She swallowed, trying to loosen the tightness of her throat as she visualized Skada's refrozen state. She lifted a palm. "Goddess Helle, what is it you want with us?"

Pain shot through her arm as Bane jerked on it at the same time Helle's voice boomed into the space around them. "Silence!"

The Goddess glared straight at Bane. "You have failed, warrior. On purpose and with blatant disregard of your oath to me."

Neva blurted. "His oath t-to you?"

Bane furrowed his brow. "Quiet, Neva. Keep silent now, for once."

She turned on him with vehemence. "Not likely, mister. You swore an oath to the Goddess Helle?"

A dark shape slithered behind Helle's eyes. "A blood oath, my dear."

"Since he's not answering, I'll ask you. With all respect, Goddess, what did he swear?"

Helle's lips slid into a sinister smile.

When Bane squeezed her shoulder, Neva shook off his touch. The fear and anger flooding her insides allowed her to maintain a firm tone. "What oath, Goddess?"

"He swore to kill you."

Her lungs squeezed tight, and she couldn't seem to get a breath. She stepped away from Bane, her heart a thudding conflagration of horror and despair.

Bane shook his fist at Helle. "Tell her the rest of it."

Helle's head tilted a fraction of an inch before she flung a flash of green light at Bane, sending him to his knees, a spasm of pain on his face. "Very well." She flicked her attention back to Neva. "He swore to kill you—before you transformed into a demoness."

Fear clawed gaping wounds in Neva's abdomen. She wanted to feel shocked, but deep within she had known of impending disaster. It resembled a train a long way off in a tunnel. At first the light bobbled dim and small. Then it loomed larger, accompanied by a noisy rumble. The end consisted of nothing but a blinding glare and an unbearable roar. Fate made escape impossible, despite the immense effort. Her breast heaved. She straightened up and stiffened her spine. "I am no demoness. Far from it."

Helle withdrew a small round object from a pocket of her gown. She held it out toward Neva.

When Neva didn't move, Helle hissed with exasperation. "Take it, Wytchfae."

Biting her lip, she took halting steps toward Helle. An unpleasant jolt of electricity shot into her as she received the object from Helle's alabaster fingers. Rather than stay close to the formidable Goddess, she scooted back near Bane. Better the betrayer she knew than the mistress of death and the afterlife.

Anguish permeated Bane's voice. "Don't look, Neva."

Dread sliding through her veins like leeches, slurping away any courage she had left, her trembling fingers guided the mirror up toward her face.

She blinked in confusion, staring at the wild eyed, frightening sight in the glass. This could not be her reflection. Skada's veins popped out from the face of a sorceress in such a loathsome fashion, not hers. She was just Neva, a plain budding Wytchfae from a small college town in Central Florida.

She flung the mirror to the ground. It crashed against a rock and shattered. A shard of glass flew up and bit into the flesh just above her breast. She jerked out the jagged edge, flinging it down and grinding it with the toe of her boot. Her spine bowed, sending her head back. Agony sucked at her shoulder blades. Her bones ground together and seemed to be trying to pierce their way out of her flesh. Biting her lip until she tasted blood, she sought to control the forces threatening to take her over. Heat flared through her body, and she drew in great gulps of air.

Bane clutched his abdomen and spoke between gasps. "Give her a chance, Goddess. Let her choose."

Neva glanced at him. Choose what? To be demon or not? She'd choose the latter in a heartbeat.

Helle's voice, metallic and distant, trickled into her consciousness as if from far away. "It's too late. Her *draugr* wings are forming. She is demoness."

What on earth did Helle mean? Neva reached around to feel her back. From her shoulder blades sharp protrusions slipped from her flesh like the finest couture. Even without being able to see them, their obsidian color flooded behind her eyes. Horror grabbed her heart, causing it to crash against her rib cage like the pounding of a great bass drum. The cry that escaped her lips did not sound human. Her eyes met Bane's, and she cringed as her own desperation was reflected back to her in his tortured gaze.

Tears of torment threatened to swamp her as Bane took a deep shuddering breath. It seemed to her that he sought a warrior's strength. His body stilled into the quiet of nonengagement. Had he concocted this warrior's trick or had Odin taught him this stoicism?

His voice when he spoke to the Goddess sounded remote, almost calm. "It's not too late, Helle."

"Why should I allow her this moment, warrior?"

"Because you can. You once chose to do the right thing. Now it's her turn. You can give her that option."

"The lunar alignment is nigh. You see her face, her wings. The girl's veins thrum with the power of her mother's demoness blood."

"Your blood flows within her too. She deserves the choice. You said she did."

"It's too late."

"Not...too late. Never. You had a chance to choose. Do what you wish with me, but give her the same opportunity—please, Goddess. It is your nature."

After a long silence, Helle released a breath that matched her icy, regal countenance. She nodded. "Very well." She waved her hand, and two swirling vortices opened against the wall. Runic inscriptions in blood red guarded each one. "Your warrior has supplicated your case, Wytchfae. Before you are two doors. One is the way of controlled power. It allows you to hold the reins of the mighty black horse and the white. The other is the way of lust and unquenchable thirst. The power there is greater than anything imaginable, but it is also uncontrollable. It will consume you, as it did your mother, my sister Skada. One path is life, the other death. Choose."

"I-I don't know."

Bane reeled toward her. "Neva, feel in your heart for the answer. Odin will guide you." His hand slipped into his shirt. He jerked a leather strap off his neck and tossed it at her feet. Then he canted words that sounded like lines from an ancient saga. He appeared to be performing a spell of some sort.

Puzzled, Neva picked up the object he had thrown to her. From the strap dangled a rune she'd never seen. She closed her fingers around it.

Alarm shattered Helle's composure. "Warrior, where did you get that magic? From Odin? Stop the incantation at once! It's her choice now." With a flick of her wrist, the Goddess sent Bane thrashing against the great craggy walls. He fell with a sickening thud.

Helle's voice boomed. "Choose!"

If Neva pondered it, she'd never be able to choose. With Bane's talisman, or Odin's, clasped in her fist tight against her heart, she ran headlong toward one of the doors. The metal in her hand heated and throbbed. The blood on the doors gushed downward, bleeding into the earth below. At the last minute she veered to the left and crashed through the other vortex. The electricity picked her up like wind and tossed her high into the air. Her ears pounded, and in a moment she could hear nothing at all. The silence of the universe filled her being, and time stood still. Then a strange beat of music sprang up in the realm of her heart. She seemed to travel through time and space, and the scarlet river of her blood crackled with the electrons and filaments of stars.

Energy greater than her own supported her. Perhaps her patron Goddess had come to her at last. She no longer had physical wings, but rather soared on those of spirit.

When she landed flat on her bottom, she looked up in shock at Helle standing over her and Bane crumpled like a rag doll against the stones. Picking herself up, she ran to him. Her breath caught at his pallor. Blood flowed from a gash on his head. The fierce warrior lay unmoving. "Bane." She slipped her arm beneath his head.

His eyes fluttered open. Without moving his head, he looked toward where the vortices were dissipating. His voice rasped. "You did it, Neva. You made the right choice."

Helle took a step toward the two of them. She waved her hand, and color reappeared in Bane's high cheekbones.

"That she did, warrior. Now what should I do with you? What will be your punishment for your disobedience and betrayal?"

"I am at your mercy, Goddess Helle."

"I suppose you are going to tell me you are proud of your actions."

His voice came out low and pain-filled, but clear enough. "Damn straight. I didn't kill the woman I have come to...come to...." He sagged as if the words sapped his strength. He looked up at Neva, and a brief but emotion laden smile flickered over his features.

Her heart sputtered at his expression, and a strange feeling of wonder swelled within her.

Helle's tone sharpened. "The woman you have come to—*what*, warrior?"

Bane encircled Neva's hands with his own. The heat from his body danced around hers.

Spellbound, she helped him rise.

His intense gaze never left her. "The woman I have come to care for beyond all reason."

Neva's lips parted in a gasp. Her hands trembled within his as she drifted closer to the safety and allure of his embrace.

He tucked her under his shoulder and bowed his head with reverence at Helle. "Thank you, Goddess, for giving her a chance. I'm ready to take my punishment."

Helle pursed her lips. "I shall think on that, warrior. It may be punishment, or I may decide upon another task for you. Perhaps for the two of you. I shall contemplate the problem at my leisure. In the meantime, go with your Wytchfae and regain your strength." In a noisy burst of light, she disappeared.

Bane cupped Neva's cheek. His whispered words were low and husky. "We haven't seen the last of her yet, but right now I don't give a damn." He groaned. "Kiss me, Wytchfae, before I die from want of you." He dragged her against his body.

She lifted her face to Bane's and stood on tiptoe to meet his lips. He enfolded her in his embrace to bestow the kind of kiss she had always dreamed about, that only he could give her. It was hot, sexy, and all consuming. It was a forever kind of kiss. She melted against her fierce warrior. The love shining from his eyes set her mind at ease. It told her all she needed to know. In his warm and protective arms, she had found home.

The End

About the Author

Flossie Benton Rogers writes action-packed paranormal fantasy romances, historical romances, and cozy mysteries. Known for conjuring the magic in romance.

Mystic adventurer, former library director and teacher. Essential Energy Balancing and Reiki master. Passionate about true love, mystical realms, mythology, astrotheology, and hidden realities. Coffee aficionado. Bedazzled thrall of Marigold the fur fae. Loves to hang out with myth, magic, and mayhem.

Visit her at:

www.flossiebentonrogers.com

Paranormal Fantasy Romance Novels
by Flossie Benton Rogers:

Runes – Wytchfae 1

Guardian of the Deep – Wytchfae 2

Mind Your Goddess – Wytchfae 3

Time Singer – Wytchfae 4

Lord of Fire – Wytchfae 5

Demoness Dreams – Wytchfae 6

Soul Weaver – Wytchfae 7

Silver's Angel – Wytchfae 8

PRINT ANTHOLOGIES:

Dark Guardians

Dark Warriors

POETRY:

Frost Fyre and Other Poems